PRAISE FOR JA
DEATH OF

"As well-planned and as subtly executed as any of the . . . earlier Superintendent Otani novels; and James Melville extracts a good deal of quiet humour from Otani's experiences of English life."

The Times Literary Supplement

"A police story of an entirely different sort . . ."

Wilson Library Bulletin

"The fourth saga of the exploits of Superintendent Otani will please his fans mightily. . . .Melville's insouciant wit and complex plot ensure suspense fans a good time."

Publishers Weekly

"One of the best in the series!"

Library Journal

"DEATH OF A DAIMYO is pleasurable . . . Melville has succeeded in filling it with a group of memorable characters and a number of interesting asides about contemporary Japanese society."

Best Sellers

Fawcett Crest Books
by James Melville:

THE CHRYSANTHEMUM CHAIN

THE NINTH NETSUKE

A SORT OF SAMURAI

WAGES OF ZEN

DEATH OF A DAIMYO

James Melville

FAWCETT CREST • NEW YORK

A Fawcett Crest Book
Published by Ballantine Books

First published in Great Britain

 Published in the United States by Ballantine Books, a division of Random House, Inc., New York.

Library of Congress Catalog Card Number: 84-11749

ISBN 0-449-20824-9

This edition published by arrangement with St. Martin's Press

Manufactured in the United States of American

First Ballantine Books Edition: February 1987

大名の死

Daimyo n. A feudal lord. (colloq.) a supreme gangster boss

THE PRINCIPAL CHARACTERS

In England

Superintendent Tetsuo OTANI	Commander, Hyogo Prefectural Police Force
Hanae OTANI	His Wife
Akiko SHIMIZU	Their daughter
Akira SHIMIZU	Her Husband
Kazuo SHIMIZU	Their son
Rosie WINCHMORE	Their baby-sitter
Chief Superintendent Fred NICKLEBY	Of Scotland Yard
Yukio NODA	First Secretary, Japanese Embassy
Detective Sergeant FARRIER	Cambridge County Police
Sir Benjamin LINCOLN	Master of St Cuthbert's College, Cambridge University
Shigeru MURAKAMI	Philanthropist
Dr Ikuo TAWARA	Physicist
Dr Kenji KUBO	Thomas Hardy specialist
Masako KUBO	His wife
Tomoko KUBO	Their daughter

In Japan

Inspector Jiro KIMURA	Acting commander, Hyogo Prefectural Police Force
Inspector 'Ninja' NOGUCHI	His colleague
Detective Patrolman Kenichi MIGISHIMA	Kimura's assistant
Detective Woman Patrolman	Criminal Investigation Dept:

Junko MIGISHIMA	married to Kenichi Migishima
Konnosuke YAMAMOTO	Supreme boss of the *Yamamotogumi* gangster syndicate
Mikio UCHIBORI	A possible successor to Yamamoto
Hideo SHIRAISHI	Another possible successor

AUTHOR'S NOTE

Hyogo is a real prefecture, and it has a police force. It should be emphasised therefore that all the characters in this story are wholly fictitious and bear no relation to any actual person, living or dead.

Prologue

KNEELING, THE GEISHA SOUNDLESSLY SLID OPEN THE paper-covered lattice of the *shoji* screens, to reveal a fat, pale moon newly risen above the eastern hills which separate Kyoto from Lake Biwa. Within a very few weeks it would be warm enough for her patron to make use of the platform built out over the glittering surface of the Kamo river, and enjoy the sounds of merry-making from similar platforms outside the other teahouses of the Pontocho geisha quarter; but tonight he stayed inside the darkened room, motionless on the deep purple brocade *zabuton* cushion, watching his mistress place her chalk-white, painted hands together and bow her head in a brief obeisance to the moon.

His left arm was placed at ease on a padded arm-rest resembling those used by the great men of Japan in former centuries, and though he wore a sober business suit rather than the elaborate robes of a *daimyo,* it was appropriate that Konnosuke Yamamoto should be in such a setting and physical attitude. The supreme boss of the dominant gangster syndicate of western Japan had all at once realised that he had not much longer to live.

The geisha had returned to his side and Yamamoto had begun to talk quietly to her about the progress at the special geisha high school of her daughter by a previous patron when he broke off in the middle of a word, and a trickle of saliva started from one corner of the leathery old mouth. The moonlight bathed the room, and the geisha swore later that she saw the shadow of death flit over the old man's withered face.

Then he slumped forward, and the geisha managed to prevent his head from banging against the gleaming lacquer surface of the low table before him, and ease him onto his back. There followed what seemed like a long period during which she simply held his hand, or rather, suffered her own to be clutched in Yamamoto's, which was quivering and sometimes contracting in muscular spasms which she found quite painful. All this time the geisha wondered dispassionately if he would die on the premises. He was, after all, seventy-eight years old.

Eventually the thin hand relaxed a little, but continued to tremble, and Yamamoto opened his eyes. It was evident that he was conscious, and as he opened his mouth she bent over to listen to him. All he whispered was "My car . . . time to go," and the geisha scrambled up and padded hurriedly over the soft, smooth *tatami* mats to the sliding door, so far forgetting her rigid professional discipline as to open it without first kneeling again. She knew that Yamamoto's hefty young driver-bodyguard would be somewhere nearby, and in fact surprised him with his hand lost in the folds of the kimono of one of the young maids of the house, a little way along the polished wooden corridor.

That circumstance in itself occasioned no embarrassment to any of the three of them, and very soon the young man was carrying his employer, drooping and only half-conscious, in his arms down the stairs, slipping into the shoes placed in readiness in the entrance hall at the bottom almost without breaking his step. The car had had to be parked more than a hundred metres away from the narrow alley of Pontocho, but the few passers-by were incurious as the little procession hurried along. Wealthy drunks are a commonplace sight in that locality, after all.

As the geisha and the maid settled the old man into the back of the car the driver went to the row of public telephones nearby and made a hasty call to Kobe. He was back at the car as the maid closed the door on her side. Leaning in from the other side, the geisha touched the old man's shoulder in a gesture which might have been affectionate. "Take care of yourself," she murmured, but Yamamoto made no reply.

Then the geisha closed the car door for her patron for the last time, and stood watching as the red tail-lights disappeared round a corner. She felt little emotion, but her brain was working fast. Although her status as Yamamoto's mistress had for years been a technicality, it was an important one to her, since it prevented her by the terms of her contract from taking another lover. In spite of this, one at least of the possible successors to the headship of the mighty *Yamamoto-gumi* had looked her over in the past year or two. It would be unfortunate to accept the wrong man as her next patron.

Although the geisha had quite expected that Yamamoto might die in the tea-house, it had not occurred to any of those involved in the incident to summon an ambulance. Nobody who knew the *daimyo* could suppose for a second that he would, given the chance, die anywhere except in his own bed, attended by his personal physician. Dr Shinobe would, the driver knew, be waiting at the house in Kobe by the time they arrived there in an hour or so. His phone call had seen to that.

Traffic was light, and within ten minutes the luxurious car was sweeping past the dark bulk of the Rashomon Gate of the Toji temple, the graceful silhouette of the pagoda within the huge temple precincts fretted in inky clarity against the silvery sky. The driver smiled to himself when he heard a familiar sound and saw in the rear-view mirror that Yamamoto had come to himself sufficiently to pick up the radio-phone in the back of the car.

He was not surprised when next the soundproof glass screen rose between them at a touch of the button at Yamamoto's side. He had anyway a pretty shrewd idea of the identity of the person whose phone would soon ring.

Chapter 1

London

VERY LITTLE NOISE FROM OUTSIDE PENETRATED INTO THE huge lavishly appointed office of the Japanese Ambassador to the Court of St James, and newly-arrived diplomats on his staff tended to lower their voices when summoned to his presence. The Counsellor in particular was almost inaudible, and for this reason his contributions to discussions were generally ignored. "I quite agree," he was saying unnecessarily, addressing himself to the Japan Airlines calendar on the pale green wall as the Minister drew his remarks to a conclusion.

"Well, then, Your Excellency, I think you need have no anxiety. It's a private visit and we should stay in the background. He's unlikely to want any help from us, and he'll be staying with his daughter and her husband, so you needn't offer any entertainment."

The Ambassador nodded with a little sigh. "That makes a change," he said wearily. "I shall have to do something for that crowd of business people coming for the opening, though. Why on earth is that fellow Murakami coming? I didn't think anybody in the Federation of Japanese Industry could stand him."

The Minister looked across at the younger man who was sitting quietly by the window, having said nothing since entering the room with his superiors. His face was expressionless and the Minister shrugged. "He offered a massive donation. So big that they had to give him a place in the visiting delegation."

"Terrible fellow, terrible fellow," the Ambassador grumbled. "The Americans put him in jail after the war, you know. Quite right, too. They should never have let him out again. Don't want him in my house." He looked at the Counsellor belligerently. "Anyway, let's get back to this wretched policeman. Otani. I find it very odd that the security people at home seem to think he may be under some threat here. Something to do with that old crook Yamamoto being on his death-bed, wasn't it?"

This time he glared at the young man by the window until he nodded in assent. "Well, then, you'd better have a quiet word with his son-in-law. He's supposed to be the go-between with the people at Cambridge over this opening ceremony business anyway, so you don't need any complicated excuse."

The Intelligence man finally opened his mouth. "I'll be at the airport anyway," he said as the Ambassador shuffled fussily through the papers on the tooled leather surface of his desk. "I've arranged for the British police to welcome him, and I can talk to Shimizu—the son-in-law—while we're waiting. The family will be there, needless to say."

His Japanese was perfectly correct but somehow inelegant, probably because he had spent many of his formative years in Britain, and the Ambassador experienced a familiar twitch of irritation at the presence of this cuckoo in his comfortable diplomatic nest, though he knew it to be unreasonable.

When his trio of subordinates left the room, the Ambassador moved over to the table against one wall, on which stood a *bonsai* miniature tree, a gnarled old pine no more than a foot high, in a ceramic bowl of palest turquoise. As he delicately stroked a clump of Lilliputian needles he reflected that it was a great honour to be assigned to London, but that the experience would be so much more enjoyable if only other eminent Japanese would stay at home.

"Go on, try one," Hanae urged the object of all the high-level anxiety. Superintendent Tetsuo Otani of the Hyogo Prefectural Police Force based in Kobe tried hard to look polite as the British Airways stewardess offered a tray of hors d'oeuvres, and pointed glumly at two or three of the items which looked reasonably palatable. The blonde girl beamed and said something in English, then turned away as Hanae carefully enunciated "Thank you" again, this time on her husband's behalf. Back at the galley in the rear of the firstclass compartment, the English girl tapped her Japanese colleague on the shoulder. "You can serve the main course, Kazuko," she said. "His wife's rather sweet, but he gives me the creeps."

The Japanese stewardess smiled patiently. "He just doesn't understand English, that's all," she said. "I was talking to him earlier. He didn't want to go to London anyway. He's never been outside Japan before. His wife persuaded him. Their daughter lives there—her husband's a businessman from Osaka managing the firm's London office. So they're going to see their grandson. He's three. Mr Otani showed me a photo."

She glanced at the swarthy man of indeterminate age now moodily chewing as the handsome woman at his side chatted happily to him, obviously herself in the highest of spirits. "I tried to find out what he does, but he wouldn't say. Must be important, but he doesn't act like a businessman. Might be some government official, I suppose. What do you think, Veronica?"

"I don't think anything," said Veronica tersely. "Still, I suppose he's an improvement on that lot in the economy class." Even over the general background noise of the plane the sound of raucous singing could be heard from the rearmost regions, where a group of twenty or so Japanese golfers were enjoying their togetherness, with their transparent plastic carrier bags bulging with cigarettes, macadamia nuts and steaks bought during the refuelling stop at Anchorage piled high on and around their seats. The friends they expected to make in England would be happy with their gifts, they hoped.

Otani brightened a little when the trolley came round with Kazuko at the controls, and he claimed untruthfully in response to her question to be enjoying his flight. In fact he had been morose from the moment he and Hanae first boarded the Jumbo at Osaka International Airport, and he had barely sorted out the bewildering paraphernalia of headphones, eyeshades, slippers, menus and other objects thrust upon him by an effusive steward by the time they reached Tokyo, where the majority of passengers boarded and where Otani briefly and insanely entertained the idea of making a run for it.

He admitted to Hanae that they had plenty of space in the first-class cabin, especially as there were only five other passengers besides themselves, and preferred not to question her too closely about how they had been able to afford to travel in such luxury.

Hanae was in charge of all their savings as well as of the day-to-day economy of their household, and when she reported with conspiratorial glee that there were remarkable deals to be had from travel agents these days, Otani let the matter drop. Hanae for her part fully intended to extract the maximum possible enjoyment from the one and only overseas trip she was likely to make in her husband's lifetime, and felt in any case that it would be unseemly for the parents-in-law of the head of the London office of one of Osaka's leading trading companies to emerge on arrival from the wrong end of the plane.

The meal over and the array of largely unused cutlery and glasses removed, Hanae settled back happily to watch the second film of the flight while Otani dozed fitfully, wondering in his more lucid moments whether he might suggest to Hanae that they should return separately to Japan. She could stay on in London, of course, but with every minute that passed he became more and more uneasy at the thought of having left Inspector Jiro Kimura in charge at his headquarters.

As though on cue, Hanae interrupted him during one such reverie by removing her headphones and glancing at him. On the screen at the front of the darkened cabin a woman in a bikini mouthed soundlessly what Otani surmised must be insults at a man standing beside her at the poolside gesticulating at an open letter. "He looks a bit like Mr Kimura, doesn't he?" Hanae said indulgently.

Although Otani frequently teased the Head of the Foreign Affairs Section of his force about his taste for imported clothes, his vanity and his incomprehensible pleasure in the company of foreigners, he had never hitherto accused him of looking like one; and Otani now blinked at his wife with some surprise. "Well, I mean he's very, well, *stylish,* don't you think?" Aware that she had laid herself open to one of Otani's withering sallies, Hanae hastily went on. "I wonder how he's enjoying being Acting Commander? It's the first time, isn't it?"

"He's been in charge before. A day or two at a time, when I've been away in Tokyo or during holidays. I've never had to make a formal appointment till now, though." He sighed. "Not necessary unless I leave Japan." Otani looked so woebegone that Hanae took his hand and squeezed it.

"I'm *sure* you'll enjoy it when you get there," she said encouragingly, then peered at her watch, already set to London time. "About four and a half hours more," she murmured. "Why don't you try to have another nap?"

She reached over and lowered the eyeshade which had been pulled up to Otani's forehead, and he obediently pretended to go to sleep, his mind hopelessly alert. He couldn't have appointed the older and immensely experienced Inspector Noguchi as Acting Commander. Ninja Noguchi was a detective of genius, but no administrator. As for the wintry Inspector Sakamoto of the CID, Otani cared not in the least how offended he was at being passed over. He just hoped, without any real confidence, that Kimura would abstain from taking any disastrous initiatives during his absence.

Miles above Labrador, the plane amounted to nothing but a tiny green blip on the air traffic controllers' radar screens. On the cinema screen in the front cabin of BA Flight 6 the man who reminded Hanae of Kimura was now in bed with the girl from the poolside. She had removed her bikini, but kept the sheets decorously tucked under her armpits as she abandoned herself to his caresses. It was an American film. Few people look good at Heathrow at six forty-five in the morning. Nevertheless, Hanae had spent a long time in the toilet in the hour before they landed, and Otani had done his best. He was at least freshly shaved, and smiled broadly as the opaque doors opened and he steered their luggage trolley through the greeting area where he saw his daughter waving like a baseball cheerleader, copied more hesitantly by his grandson, perched on the shoulders of Akira Shimizu.

Brief chaos ensued as Hanae snatched the little boy and Shimizu took charge of the trolley, which like all those at London Airport had a pronounced tendency to veer off to one side. Akiko, to his surprised pleasure, actually kissed her father warmly on the cheek. "You look—English," Otani said incredulously as he seized her by the shoulders and looked her up and down.

It was not really true, even though at thirty-two Akiko Shimizu was quite big for a Japanese woman, and the fashionable cropped hair-style by Vidal Sassoon was unlike anything she would have been likely to achieve in Kobe. Moreover she was wearing beige raw-silk bermuda shorts and a deep turquoise silk tunic which would have stopped the traffic in provincial Japan. All the same, there was no mistaking the eyes and mouth she had inherited from Hanae, or the crooked smile which had never quite disappeared even during her most rebellious moments as a girl. If she had a strength and authority in her manner unusual in a woman of her age and race it was Otani himself who was partly to blame.

Akiko did no more than grin by way of reply as Shimizu urged the little party to one side, into a backwater created by the flow of arriving passengers and those who had come to meet them. Otani was by then busy re-introducing himself to his grandson, and did not at first notice the two men who stepped forward as if for inspection.

Shimizu tapped him on the shoulder. He had never been able to bring himself to address Otani as "Father" and did not do so now. "Excuse me," he said loudly. Otani looked round and was startled to see a tall young Englishman beaming at him. At his side was a Japanese wearing slacks and a sweater with a suede jacket worthy of Kimura himself.

The much taller man was in a black uniform which marked him off at once to Otani as a police officer. Otani had no knowledge of British badges of rank, but it was clear to him from the leather gloves the young man held in one hand and his whole style and bearing that he was of superior status.

Satisfied that he had Otani's attention, the officer saluted impressively, his smile lodged firmly on his huge face, and emitted a stream of gibberish. The other stranger interpreted. "This is Inspector Bradshaw of the Metropolitan Police. He says he would like to welcome Superintendent and Mrs Otani on behalf of his superiors, and to express the hope that you will enjoy your stay in Britain. Chief Superintendent Nickleby apologises for not being able to be here in person, but hopes you'll have time while in London for him to show you round Scotland Yard.'

Gratified, Otani took the hand extended to him and shook it as Hanae looked on, if possible even more pleased than her husband. "There is no excuse for the trouble I have caused you in occasioning the bother of your coming to greet me notwithstanding your busy schedule," said Otani in the correct clichés of polite Japanese, then bowed once or twice to get rid of the effect of the handshake as the interpreter put his remarks into what sounded to Otani like very laconic English phrases.

"I had the honour of meeting Chief Superintendent Nickleby some years ago when he attended an Interpol meeting in Kyoto in Japan. He gave me a necktie," Otani added proudly, thanking his lucky stars that he had thought to remind Hanae to pack it in his suitcase. After this had been rendered into English while Hanae modestly stared at the FIRST CLASS tags on their luggage and young Kazuo tugged in boredom at his father's jacket, there was a brief silence during which the interpreter stepped forward.

"My name is Noda," he said with the sketchiest of bows. Of the Japanese Embassy in London. My Ambassador also asks me to welcome you in his name."

"We are most grateful for your kindness," Hanae murmured faintly, overwhelmed by the grandeur of it all. Then the English police officer cleared his throat thunderously, straightened his tie and saluted again before pointing vaguely towards the exit.

They all trailed along more or less together, Shimizu wrestling with the recalcitrant trolley, and Otani seized an opportunity to whisper to Akiko. "Are they coming with us?" he demanded in some agitation, and she shook her head reassuringly.

"Only as far as the car." As it turned out, Inspector

Bradshaw accompanied them only to the outside of the building where he saluted again, made an indecisive noise half-way to articulate speech, hestitated, then marched smartly off.

During this performance Noda lit a cigarette which he then held by one end as though it were an abbreviated conductor's baton, and as soon as the police officer had disappeared round a corner he aimed it at Otani. "Your son-in-law has some information for you," he said curtly. "Please follow his advice." Then he too was gone, and the look in Otani's eye as he turned to Shimizu was professional rather than personal.

Chapter 2

Kobe

IT TOOK A LOT TO SURPRISE NINJA NOGUCHI, BUT HE stopped short in the open doorway of the office of the Commander of the Hyogo Prefectural Police Force, and it took a full ten seconds for him to activate his vocal chords. "And what the hell do you think you're playing at?" he croaked at length.

Inspector Jiro Kimura gazed at him with an air of lofty dignity. He was, for the first time since the funeral of the last Governor of Hyogo prefecture some five years earlier, resplendent in full uniform, his cap and gloves laid tidily to one side of the desk. Without waiting for an answer, Noguchi kicked the door shut behind him and ambled towards his usual easy chair beside the coffee table. This placed him with his back to Kimura, and Noguchi settled himself with a noisy sigh, waiting for the much younger man to join him.

Noguchi himself was dressed in his usual lamentable fashion, in an old pair of trousers formerly part of a suit and which were overly roomy even for his massive hindquarters, a workman's flannel shirt, and, in deference to the warm May weather, his sagging cotton jacket in one pocket of which he generally carried a half bottle of Suntory Red whisky.

Inspector Hachiro Noguchi was immensely proud of his nickname, and frequently viewed with gloomy pleasure the television programmes which dealt with the improbable exploits of the historical *ninja,* the spy-assassins employed by the contending warlords of centuries earlier, whose agility and ingenuity led to a superstitious belief on the part of the common people that they were magicians who could render themselves invisible at will.

Although Kimura was one of those who genuinely marvelled at Noguchi's ability to lose himself in the less savoury courts and alleys of Kobe and to pass unnoticed among the day-labourers and layabouts of the waterfront, he found him all too conspicuous in the office; so conceding defeat in the small battle of wills, he rose nimbly to his feet and crossed the room to sit opposite Noguchi.

"That's not your chair," Noguchi snapped immediately. It was the one habitually occupied by Otani during their conferences. Kimura looked at him for a long moment, then with a shrug changed to his own usual place. Noguchi was not quite old enough to be his father and they enjoyed a bantering relationship based on genial expressions of contempt on Noguchi's part and injured innocence on Kimura's, but there were times when it was beyond human capacity to withstand the old thug's sheer authority of character.

"No need to be like that, Ninja," Kimura complained as the silence extended itself awkwardly. "He *did* appoint me Acting Commander, you know."

What passed for a smile briefly disturbed the crags and crevices of Noguchi's battered face. "Fat chance any of us will be able to forget it. I know he did. I told him to. Didn't tell you to get yourself up like that, though, did he?"

Kimura looked down at his carefully pressed navy-blue

trousers. Although after taking delivery of his uniform from the appointed police tailor he had at once handed it over to the high-class Chinese establishment in Tor Road for alterations and minor improvements, in his heart of hearts he was beginning to regret putting it on that day. There was a coarseness about the material which made him feel itchy, and in any case even his boundless self-esteem had not been proof against the ill-concealed grins of the patrolmen and administrative staff whom he had encountered on his way into the building and up to Otani's office on the first floor, past the walls lined with photographs of former commanders of the force.

He could think of no suitable rejoinder, and was relieved when the subject was changed. "It's true," Noguchi said abruptly, after poking his finger into one ear and inspecting his findings. "Couple of days or so, they reckon." There had been no particular secret about the illness of Konnosuke Yamamoto: indeed it had been reported in most of the newspapers, along with a certain amount of careful speculation about its implications. GANG BOSS GRAVELY ILL, the headlines chirruped blithely, unconcerned like all Japanese papers about the risk of a libel action.

Indeed, before Otani left for London the three of them had talked briefly about the matter. Yamamoto's headquarters was in Osaka and thus within the jurisdiction of Otani's opposite number in the Osaka police, but he lived in the Hyogo area so in theory the two forces were in constant contact about Yamamoto's activities. "Ah," said Kimura, leaning forward keenly. "Interesting. The Chief thought he'd probably pull through again. He had a stroke a couple of years ago, of course. Was this another one?"

Noguchi shook his head economically. "Everything packing up, doctor says. Wants him in the hospital, but Yamamoto won't go."

"Listen, Ninja, I've been thinking," Kimura announced, and Noguchi raised his eyes to heaven, at which

Kimura exploded. "Damn it, Inspector," he barked unforgivably. "Whether or not you recommended it and whether or not you like it, I have been placed in temporary command at this headquarters, and I have certain responsibilities! I may also have certain instructions for you."

Kimura had gone too far and he knew it as soon as the brief blaze of anger had expended itself. Although Noguchi did not move a muscle, Kimura felt the almost physical quality of the emanation from him. When Noguchi did speak, his voice was mild. The effect was all the more chilling. "Don't ever talk to me like that again, son," he said. "And don't act like a stupid jumped-up *tofu*-brained ticket collector, even if you do dress up like one." Kimura was humbled, and was also honest enough to realise that his uniform *did* somewhat resemble those seen at the ticket barriers of railway stations.

"I'm sorry, Ninja," he said generously. "Truly sorry. That was a stupid thing to say. Look, you know I need your help to cope with all this while the Chief's out of the country. Don't jump on me every time you disagree with the way I go about things." The quality of the silence with which Noguchi heard this speech was quite different from before. Eventually he nodded, and both men knew that all was again well between them.

"You've been thinking," Noguchi conceded eventually.

Kimura nodded. "Yes. About the time the Chief went to see Yamamoto in his office."

"On his own," Noguchi confided grimly. "He was a mug to do that."

"Well, it worked out. He got what he wanted from him," Kimura argued. "Anyway, you remember he said he might go and see him again one day, to try to find out what's likely to happen—I mean who'll take over when Yamamoto dies. What I thought was, that since the Chief won't be back for nearly two weeks, if old Yamamoto's really on the way out this time, well, that *we* ought to go and see him.''

Noguchi suppressed the blistering comment that rose unbidden to his lips and decided instead to keep the peace. ''Doubt if it could be done,'' was all he actually said.

''It wasn't too easy to organise the other meeting, but you managed it,'' Kimura pointed out.

''He wasn't on his deathbed then,'' said Noguchi tersely, but fell into a reverie which Kimura found encouraging as he waited quietly.

''It would be a challenge,'' he suggested craftily after a while.

Noguchi merely grunted.

''Can't see the point,'' he said then, opening one eye. ''Past caring by now. Must be. We'll know soon enough when there's a new boss.''

''I grant you that. But there could be some blood, wouldn't you say? Some shooting here and there before the dust settles. If we knew who Yamamoto had designated we might be able to head it off.'' Kimura shrugged. ''Still, if you don't think you can fix it for us . . . it was just a thought.''

''Didn't say that,'' came the instant reaction Kimura had hoped for. ''Got hold of the doctor easy enough. Might be able to work something.''

During the lengthy process of getting himself to his feet while avoiding too much pressure on the arm which had been weakened when he was shot the previous year on board a Korean freighter in Kobe Harbour, Noguchi was obviously already pondering ways and means, and Kimura had the sense not to interrupt. ''See you later, perhaps,'' was all he said as he accompanied Noguchi to the door, before returning to the desk to scan the reports from divisional headquarters throughout the huge area policed by the Hyogo force.

A multiple suicide in Himeji looked as if it might call

for special investigation, and yet another forged five-thousand yen note had turned up at the race-track. A couple of hours passed almost without his noticing, and Kimura became absorbed in an account of a computer embezzlement by a young woman bank clerk who had contrived to relieve her employers of the equivalent of approximately fifty years' salary, only to hand it over to her married lover who promptly absconded with it.

When the telephone rang it took him a moment to focus his attention on what Noguchi at the other end of the line was saying, but then after a hasty glance at his newest watch, which incorporated a calculator, a perpetual calendar and an additional time indicator which he had set to London time in deference to Otani, Kimura quickly agreed to what was being suggested.

Kimura always kept a variety of plain clothes available at the office, and he now changed very quickly out of the contentious uniform and into the sober grey business suit on the bent wire hanger suspended from the old-fashioned umbrella stand in the corner. The new white shirt and dull green silk tie he had recently bought from the Turnbull and Asser boutique in the Seibu Department Store after learning that James Bond favoured this particular London shirt-maker. He was pleased with the ensemble, which contributed, he thought, to an effect of quiet dignity, entirely appropriate to the occasion.

As he made his way downstairs again to the main entrance, Kimura wondered idly what Ninja would do about his own appearance, and was simultaneously shocked and oddly reassured to discover him looking exactly the same as during their stormy conference earlier. Nevertheless, there was no mistaking the satisfaction in Noguchi's voice as he admitted that it had taken a few phone calls, but that they were expected in forty-five minutes at the Yamamoto stronghold on the outskirts of the Nada suburb of Kobe.

They were driven in an unmarked car by a sharp-faced

young plainclothesman who to Kimura's eyes made an entirely convincing gangster, while in the front passenger seat was an older man, a senior patrolman who was the nearest thing to a deputy Noguchi would admit to.

"I haven't had any lunch," Kimura complained all at once as the penetrating smell wafted in through the open windows of the car from the curry-rice bar they were passing.

They were making good time, but Noguchi shook his cruelly cropped and grizzled head decisively. "Don't want to be late," he growled, and Kimura turned to gaze disconsolately at the office workers coming and going from the many other small restaurants which lined the street they were in.

"It's not as though old Yamamoto's planning to go anywhere," he grumbled briefly, but without hope of persuading Noguchi to change his mind and stop for a bite on the way. Besides, Kimura was quite well aware of the tension in the atmosphere, and felt both elated and hesitant, as though about to go to bed with a new woman friend for the first time.

With a conscious effort he turned away from the window and stared instead at Noguchi. "What are we going to *say* to him?" he blurted out, suddenly appalled at his temerity in suggesting the idea in the first place. The driver and the other man in front affected not to hear what he said, but Kimura nevertheless at once regretted his too-obvious demonstration of nerves.

"You'll think of something," said Noguchi comfortably. "Never known you lose your tongue. Pass the time of day. Ask him what he's put in his will. Nothing to it."

At this the shoulders of the middle-aged man in the front seat heaved perceptibly, and Kimura closed his lips in a tight line and said no more. The driver had meantime negotiated a number of turns, and they were just passing the entrance to a temple, offering a glimpse of calm austerity after the bustle of the shopping streets and three- and four-storey "mansion" apartment blocks in which better-off people were increasingly choosing to live.

The massive iron-studded wooden gates of the temple were open beneath their ponderous carved wooden roof, but a simple bamboo trellis barrier no more than a couple of feet high was in place, indicating that entry by that route was forbidden to casual passers-by. At either side of a stoneflagged pathway were massive stone lanterns, and meticulously trimmed azalea bushes led the eye softly towards the main hall of the temple, approached by a flight of wooden steps. The inner paper-covered *shoji* screens were closed, and there was no sign of human life within the precincts.

"Yamamoto's parish temple," Noguchi remarked surprisingly. "Be a sight to see when they have the funeral." Kimura still held his peace, though he was tempted to ask questions. It came as a surprise to him to realise that Yamamoto was a local man. Kimura was as devoid of religious impulses as he was of highbrow cultural interests, but like all Japanese he took it for granted that when he himself died, funeral services would be held at the Kimura family temple. This was in Tokyo, even though Kimura himself had been born in Manchuria and spent a number of childhood years after the war in Chicago where his diplomat father was assigned.

The car moved on up a narrow one-way street, the driver dextrously avoiding a youth careering down it on a bicycle, steering with one hand while with the other he balanced aloft a pile of five or six well-worn lacquer lunch boxes he was clearly on the way to deliver. The district in which old Yamamoto lived was of a prosperous middle-class kind, and had something of the sense still clinging to it of the village it had once been, and probably not much more than thirty or forty years before.

There was no grand approach to the house, which stood in the small street near to a coffee bar called "Miami";

and no way for the uninformed to identify it. Indeed the house itself was quite invisible behind a formidably high wall, and the only way in was through a pair of massive black metal gates, over which a closed-circuit TV camera was mounted.

Still, the police driver had scarcely to check his speed, for while they were still several metres away the ponderous metal panels began to rumble open and to disappear on the tracks which led to their housing on each side, disclosing a paved area in which were already parked a black Mercedes and a huge maroon Cadillac. Even so, there was still room for their own Nissan Bluebird, and even an electrically operated turntable which began to move as soon as they were fairly in place, turning the car to face the gates which had by then already been closed again.

"Reminding us of the way out," Noguchi remarked cheerfully to Kimura as they clambered out of the car. "You stay here," he added in an aside to his assistant. The driver was in any case still in his seat, had taken a lurid comic book out of the glove compartment and was leafing through it with an ostentatious display of unconcern which Kimura quite envied.

"That Cadillac," Kimura murmured as quietly as he could. "Do you suppose Shiraishi's here?"

Noguchi's fleshy shoulders moved a fraction of an inch. For him this was tantamount to an extravagant shrug. "Wouldn't be surprised. Looks like his wheels."

Not for the first time since setting out, Kimura was tempted to suggest a postponement, but became aware that another man had appeared on the forecourt. He was far from young, and was dressed with such elegant sobriety that he quite outshone Kimura, at whom he was staring with distaste. "I advised him not to see you," he complained in a thin, sour voice.

"Doing your job, Doctor," Noguchi said, all tolerant good humour. "Not your fault he's a stubborn old goat."

The withering look of disapproval was transferred to Noguchi. "As you know, Inspector, I have always collaborated with the police."

"Know what's good for you, don't you?" Kimura had seldom seen Noguchi looking so pleased with himself, and concluded that he too must be excited at the thought of penetrating into the very heart of the Yamamoto domains. "Dr Shinobe—I'd like you to meet Acting Commander Kimura of the Hyogo police Force." Though only mock-courteous, Noguchi's introduction was so formal that Kimura and the doctor bowed to each other quite involuntarily and murmured the conventional phrases, to Noguchi's even greater satisfaction.

Dr Shinobe made a small sound of irritation and turned aside. "Come in, then, come in," he bleated angrily, and led the way to the house, which from outward appearances was built in the purest Japanese style. On entering, however, Kimura saw that in fact the lobby and reception rooms were furnished in Western fashion and at considerable expense though as they were led round a corner it became clear that the house formed a quadrangle. On the far side, beyond a beautiful formal garden which looked cool and green in the afternoon sunshine, was a suite of *tatami*-matted rooms.

The doctor led them round, past two sides of the garden, then slipped off his own shoes as he entered a highly polished wooden corridor. The others followed suit, Kimura puzzling over the apparent absence of bodyguards or other attendants, and Shinobe eventually paused outside a closed *fusuma* sliding door and announced his name. There was a reply, which Kimura failed to catch, upon which the doctor slid the door open and stepped in. Kimura and Noguchi followed.

Yamamoto had evidently decided to interview the police in style.

Chapter 3

London

HANAE PICKED NERVOUSLY AT THE HUGE LUMP OF PATÉ which sat like a toad on the single lettuce leaf on her plate, noticing with selfless pleasure that her husband seemed to be enjoying the atmosphere at Granny's Restaurant much more than she was. Hanae was in fact in a condition of mild cultural shock, largely brought on by their arrival at the spacious flat the Shimizus occupied at St John's Wood, in an opulent block in a broad, tree-lined avenue at least five times wider than the average street in even a well-to-do residential area in urban Japan.

Hanae had of course been in Western-style accommodation many times before, but nevertheless accompanied her daughter on a tour of inspection with mounting amazement at the luxuriousness of the furniture and fittings, the enormous rooms and in particular the spectacular appointments in the kitchen. She rooted about happily enough in the cupboards for a while, but then began to find the unfamiliarity of the goods stored there curiously threatening. The fact that Akiko did not possess an electric rice cooker struck her as odd in the extreme, and Hanae had begun to feel thoroughly at odds with life by the time Akiko sensed her exhaustion and packed her off to take a bath and try to sleep for a while.

Meantime Otani had been closeted with Shimizu in his study for nearly an hour, until Shimizu had to leave again for his office. He emerged looking thoughtful but cheerful, and later on elected to remain at the flat with the increasingly uninhibited heir to the Shimizus while Akiko went shopping by herself. Later the time difference overcame him and he too began nodding and drooping just as Hanae woke up, much more her usual self after her nap. In spite of his generalised dislike for Western-style beds Otani then achieved a solid four hours' sleep and was now attacking his own paté with relish.

The restaurant was quite small in size with places for no more than twenty diners in all, at tables ranged along the two side walls. Oval-framed Edwardian sepia photographs of ladies in enormous hats and with Wagnerian bosoms hung by way of decoration on the heavy, flocked wine-red wallpaper. Fortunately both Akiko and her husband seemed to have achieved a satisfactory command of English and Shimizu in particular had been greeted effusively by the English girl who showed them to their table and distributed copies of the menu. Hanae could read printed English a little, but this document was hand-written with such elegance that she could make neither head nor tail of it, and fell back on Akiko's advice that Farmhouse Chicken Treat was the thing to choose as a main course. Otani for his part was guided by Shimizu, who gave their orders to the girl he addressed familiarly as Emma.

Emma was a tall, well-built young woman who was dressed in Edwardian style, in a high-necked, long dress in a design of tiny flowers. Her soft brown hair, of a silkiness Hanae could only wonder at, was piled high on her head and though she had none of the frenzied enthusiasm of a Japanese waitress, she moved economically and gracefully as she coped singlehanded with all the dozen or so customers in the place. This, Shimizu explained in an undertone after Emma had retreated with their orders, was because she was really a dancer, working between engagements as many actresses, actors and dancers did in London. Since probably eighty per cent of Japanese waiters and waitresses in restaurants other than family concerns are students working their way through college, the information was interesting rather than sensational to the visitors.

"Don't you like it, Mother?"

Hanae guiltily took another morsel of the highly-seasoned paté and washed it down with an incautiously large mouthful of wine, the tears coming to her eyes as she tried not to splutter. "It's delicious," she lied bravely at last. "There is rather a lot of it, though. I suppose I'm not very hungry after the flight. Are you *sure* Kazu-chan will be all right?" Hanae herself had not been out in the evening even once during the whole of Akiko's childhood. This was the common experience of middle-class women of her generation, and though she accepted that times had changed even in Japan, the idea of leaving the three-year-old son in the care of a cheerful but unquestionably scruffy student called Rosie had appalled Hanae.

"Oh, don't worry," Akiko said calmly, having disposed of the last of her paté. "Rosie's very reliable. She's studying Japanese at London University. Kazu-chan likes her. Doesn't he?" The question was addressed to her husband, who was carrying on a private conversation with Otani.

"What?" Akira Shimizu looked first at Akiko, then at Hanae's plate, and signalled to the statuesque Emma, who came and removed everybody's after confirming solicitously that Hanae really didn't want any more.

"Really, you might be a bit more sociable," Akiko complained. "You'll be busy for days after tonight with all your visitors, and here you are boring Father and ignoring Mother."

Shimizu was unperturbed by his wife's complaint. "You see how she bullies me?" He appealed to Hanae for support. "All I was doing was explaining about the opening ceremony. For the Nantemo Institute of Japanese Studies at Cambridge University. I've fixed it so that you're both invited."

After glancing in apology to Otani he began from the beginning again, refilling all their glasses with red wine as he spoke, starting with Hanae's to her amazement. "Ladies first in England," he said courteously. "You probably saw in the Japanese papers that a group of companies and foundations has put together a lot of money to give to Cambridge to promote Japanese studies the way the Nissan car people did for Oxford."

Hanae nodded. She had seen nothing of the kind. "Well, my company's one of them, and our office here in London has been responsible for all the detailed arrangements for the transfer of the funds and so on. About half a dozen company and foundation presidents are due to arrive tomorrow for the opening ceremony on Thursday, and I thought you'd enjoy the chance to see the famous old colleges."

At this point Emma returned, and Hannae gaped at the mountain of food on the plate now laid in front of her. She was quite fond of European food, and on her occasional shopping expeditions from their suburban home at Rokko to Kobe usually treated herself to lunch at one of the many foreign restaurants there. Kobe establishments, however, followed practice elsewhere in Japan in that portions were of modest size. A six-ounce steak would be accompanied by perhaps two baby carrots, a teaspoonful of spinach and three french-fries lying in a neat row, sometimes each with a little seaweed lifebelt round the middle.

Hanae was now confronted by a gigantic half-chicken surmounted by mushrooms and accompanied by what looked like half a kilo or so of mashed potatoes, while

Otani addressed himself heartily to a whole steak and kidney pie in its own fair-sized brown dish as well as a pile of cabbage, roast potatoes and a huge stuffed tomato. Surprisingly to Hanae, Otani seemed to be absorbing the initial impact of English ways with much more pleasure than she, but she consoled herself with the reflection that it was after all only their first evening, and that her stomach would no doubt adjust to such assaults in due course.

She picked gingerly at one edge of the chicken, skilled enough at handling the enormous knife and fork, but thinking wistfully of tiny fragments of fish or Japanese pickle, small enough to constitute a single modest mouthful when raised to the lips with wooden chopsticks. Unlike her mother, Akiko tucked into her Farmhouse Chicken Treat with gusto, and the food and wine brought an attractive colour to her cheeks.

''Who was that rude man Noda?'' she now enquired abruptly. ''I thought diplomats were supposed to be polite. Surely the Foreign Ministry ought to choose its best people for London?''

This was not the first time Otani had noticed Akiko being snobbish about her new country of residence. ''Of the same quality as you and Akira-kun here?'' he suggested with an air of innocence, and she might have blushed, but perhaps it was the effect of the wine.

''No, you know what I mean,'' Akiko protested as Otani continued to gaze at her, having noticed the guarded expression on Shimizu's face and giving him time to choose his words.

''Noda-san *is* a bit unusual,'' he admitted at last. ''In the first place he was brought up here, and actually his English is better than his Japanese. He sometimes has trouble reading Chinese characters. He acts as a kind of—well, liaison man, I suppose you could say. Also interprets for Japanese VIPs such as the eminent Superintendent here,'' he added with a smile. ''In fact, he's very kindly offered to go with you to Scotland Yard when you make your call on Chief Superintendent Nickleby. My English isn't nearly good enough, and besides, I've got to take care of all my visitors. Noda-san will be coming to Cambridge too."

Otani already knew of this arrangement, but a momentary panic now seized him. "How will I get there?" he demanded. "Will Noda come to your *manshon* for me?" Emma the hostess/waitress discreetly took Hanae's virtually untouched plate of food away first, then removed the other, empty dishes. Hanae felt better immediately.

"No, he'll meet you there," Shimizu said. "Don't worry, though, I've arranged for Rosie to take you. She lives quite near us, and she doesn't have a class that morning. Her Japanese is rather halting but she'll understand you pretty well and she certainly won't lose you on the way to Scotland Yard."

Otani rather liked the idea of having a young woman as escort, and sat back and eyed with interest the trolley which Emma now brought alongside. It was a long time since he had eaten so much, but like all Japanese he had a sweet tooth and he demanded from Akiko a full explanation in Japanese of each of the confections Emma now displayed and named.

Hanae settled with relief for fresh fruit salad, while Otani opted for a Chocolate Pot, allowing Emma to anoint the sticky brown lump of calories with cream so that it looked a little like Mount Fuji in winter. Shimizu chose Lemon Meringue Pie while Akiko ordered something called Tipsy Cake, which determined Hanae to speak to her daughter seriously about her figure. It was a subject they had never discussed in Akiko's youth when as a student she had been a passionately extreme adherent of the Maoist group headed by Shimizu. Marriage and Shimizu's swift advancement in his career as a capitalist manager had not made Akiko any less of a feminist, but she did nowadays take an interest in fashion, and had already promised to take Hanae to *Comme des Enfants* where she bought her trendy expensive clothes, and round the other Bond Street and Knightsbridge shops.

It was as Otani was finishing the last of his deliciously gooey dessert that the proprietor reached them in the course of his stately round of the modest premises, and greeted Shimizu by name. His behaviour was indeed regally proprietorial even though the cashmere sweater and sports jacket struck Hanae as being inappropriate, especially on a man who must have been seventy if he was a day. She liked his bright blue eyes and plummy voice, though, and nodded and smiled in response as he addressed a series of gracious remarks to her, none of which she understood. He seemed pleased, and limped in a distinguished way back to his perch in a cubbyhole at the rear of the restaurant, after presenting each of them with a beer mat bearing the likenesses of Prince Charles and Princess Diana as though they were objects of considerable intrinsic value.

They left Granny's Restaurant soon after nine-thirty, which Shimizu claimed to be early but Hanae considered an extremely advanced hour, after Shimizu had paid the bill not in cash but by means of a cheque, which he explained were in common use in England, unlike Japan. He also delivered a tedious homily on the way home in the car on the subject of tipping, explaining that he had added fifteen per cent to the amount of the bill as a tribute to the services of Emma, and that the Otanis must remember to tip taxi drivers as well as opening the door for themselves, since the driver-operated mechanisms universal in Japanese taxis were unknown in Britain.

Otani was nodding off and paid little attention, and after a little while even Hanae was moved to change the subject by expressing the anxious hope that little Kazuo was safe and well. It proved on their arrival at St John's Wood that he had survived the ordeal of being deserted by his mother for three hours, and was fast asleep in bed clutching a large soft Snoopy with one ear missing. Rosie for her part was surrounded by Japanese dictionaries and looked harassed wearing her glasses and still clutching the magnifying glass she was using to help her decipher the small print of her text.

As she and Akiko talked together in English, Otani glanced at the book, a novel by Natsume Soseki which he had himself been required to read as a boy in the high school attached to Osaka University where his father was then a professor. He felt a twinge of sympathy for Rosie and confirmed in very clear and carefully enunciated Japanese exactly what time he would be leaving with her on the day of his appointment with Chief Superintendent Nickleby. Then she was gone with Shimizu who was to drive her home.

"I'm sure her mother will be very worried about her being out so late," Hanae said. "It's nearly half-past ten."

Akiko laughed out loud and wagged her head at the impossibility of explaining. "This isn't Japan you know, Mother," she said at last. "Rosie's parents are divorced and have both re-married. They live in completely different parts of England. Rosie shares a small apartment with a very nice boy called Roger. He has a beard and works as a bus conductor."

"Oh," said Hanae weakly. It was clearly time to go to bed.

Chapter 4
Cambridge

OTANI AND HANAE STOOD WARILY TOGETHER NEAR THE open french windows which led to the exuberantly colourful garden of the Master's Lodge at St Cuthbert's College, Cambridge. Hanae would have liked nothing better than to go out into the gentle May sunshine of England and explore, especially as it seemed that this was one of those English gardens she had read about, intended for people to walk about in rather than to contemplate from inside the house. She had never seen so many different flowers growing in the same place at the same time before, or grass of such a brilliant green. Everybody else was still in the enormous book-lined study, though, and Hanae dared not make the first move.

It had been a morning of surprises. Hanae had been luxuriating in the bath when Otani, already up and about, was called to the telephone by Akiko. It was amazing enough that the Shimizu's flat in London had a second bathroom anyway, and moreover one which led directly off the bedroom in which they were ensconced. Still more remarkable was the size and fluffiness of the towels provided, and the fact that there was a quite separate shower cabinet which Otani, after one look at the peacock-blue bath, decided to use for his own ablutions.

Then the drive, in a hire car with a pleasant, fresh-faced young woman driver who kept up a steady flow of informative comment as she drove them through places with strange names like Epping and Woodford and thence to Cambridge. At least, Hanae supposed it must be informative, though she couldn't understand a word of it and soon ran out of the few English phrases she had memorised. By saying "Oh, really?" or "Very interesting" from time to time, however, she managed to keep her end up, quite overcoming the nervousness she had felt about being bereft of the guidance of her daughter or her son-in-law. Otani for his part remained silent and plunged in thought throughout the drive.

As soon as they arrived in the city Hanae decided that Cambridge was splendid, and she roused her husband from his reverie and made him look out of the window as they passed along Trumpington Street, admiring Corpus Christi on their right and St Catherine's on their left. In another ten minutes their driver drew up with a flourish outside the entrance to the Master's Lodge at St Cuthbert's, and the Otanis made their way with some awe towards the entrance of what to Hanae looked more like a church or medieval castle as seen on television in Japan than a house in which someone actually lived.

Shimizu was waiting for them, a smile on his lean, intelligent face. "Did you have an enjoyable drive? You must be tired," he said cheerfully, then, interpreting the anxious look on his mother-in-law's face, "Don't worry, there are plenty of people here who can speak Japanese."

It turned out to be true. There were a dozen or so people in the beautiful room which smelt of furniture polish and flowers, including two or three women; and half of them were in any case Japanese. It was the tall old Englishman in the middle who was easily the most interesting, though, since when Shimizu led the Otanis over to him to make introductions he greeted them in courteous old-fashioned Japanese of such formality that even Otani, who still seemed curiously detached from everything about him, pulled himself together and looked with interest at the Master of St Cuthbert's.

Professor Sir Benjamin Lincoln was in any case an impressive figure since over his dark suit he wore a red silk robe which gave him a priestly appearance, and he had the bushiest white eyebrows Otani had ever seen. "How good of you and your gracious consort to join us here today," he said in Japanese. "I am quite sure that you must have had a long and troublesome journey to reach this inconvenient and unpropitious region."

"Not at all," Otani responded politely. wondering if he could believe his ears.

"I say unpropitious, Madam," Sir Benjamin continued, "because Cambridge lies to the north-east of London, and I fear that you have not had time to take the circuitous route which would most certainly have been prescribed for such a journey in the Heian period, for example. But then there was less hustle and bustle a thousand years ago. At least we have selected if not a day of Maximum peace for our little ceremony, an auspicious day of the Friend-pulling character."

"You speak Japanese," announced Otani, making Hanae blush for him. It was astonishing that the old man seemed to know all about Japanese superstitions. Otani had no idea whether it was indeed a so-called Friend-pulling day, and intended to check in his diary at the earliest opportunity.

"A few words, a few words only. You are most courteous to make the effort to understand me, my dear Otani-san. I look forward to a more leisurely conversation with you before long."

It was a stylish dismissal, and Hanae and Otani were by the french windows with glasses of sherry before they quite knew what was happening, watching the Master deal equally adroitly with another new arrival, a short, tubby Japanese whom, from his air of self-importance, Otani judged to be one of the philanthropic businessmen who had put up the money.

"Are you feeling all right?" Hanae enquired suddenly, seeing that Otani had again relapsed into the reflectiveness from which he had only briefly emerged when listening to the Master.

"What? Oh, yes, yes, I'm fine. Interesting man, isn't he?" Just then three ladies bore down on Hanae and Otani was able to detach himself unobtrusively and drift out into the garden, the better to analyse once more the report he had received that morning over the telephone from Kimura.

It was the fact that old Yamamoto was not in bed when Kimura and Noguchi called on him which seemed to obsess Kimura, who mentioned it in terms of incredulity at least four times during the call, which he was careful to point out was made on Noguchi's advice. What Kimura did not say was that Noguchi had demanded that an oral report should be given to Otani, the alternative being that he, Noguchi, would himself refer the information received from Yamamoto to the Criminal Investigation Division of the National Police Agency in Tokyo.

Although he had never visited Yamamoto's house Otani could easily visualise the scene, with the dying gang boss grotesquely got up in full formal Japanese dress, propped up in a parody of the kneeling position in a quiet *tatami*-matted room, flanked by one of the better-known of his subordinates, the man Shiraishi, and by his own bodyguard. As Kimura had gone on to describe the initial wary exchanges it was as though Otani could see the wizened bald death's-head above the fine silk of the kimono and intercept the flashes of cunning which still from time to time illuminated the drugged eyes.

Nor was it difficult to share Kimura's impression of the ill-concealed impatience of Shiraishi, the fidgeting, sweating man in the expensive but too-tight suit who needed Yamamoto's formal endorsement before he could even attempt to claim the allegiance of the other seven barons who constituted what they themselves referred to as the "presidium" of the huge empire of crime and racketeering; and of Shiraishi's consternation when Yamamoto abruptly dismissed him and indicated to his bodyguard and the doctor that he wished to speak in privacy with the two police officers.

It was this part of the conversation which Otani made Kimura repeat, questioning him sharply about it before reluctantly putting the phone down and considering seriously the possibility of returning to Japan by the first available plane. Yamamoto's *actual words*, Otani had insisted, and now in the tranquil garden in Cambridge it was as though he could hear again the voice he remembered so well from their only face-to-face encounter, when Yamamoto showed him the officer's sword of his son, killed in the war, and Otani realised that he was mad.

"Shiraishi thinks he's the one," the thin voice had whispered with a hideous attempt at a cackle as Kimura and Noguchi approached him and knelt to catch his words. "So does Uchibori down there in Hiroshima." A long pause. "You should have sent Otani. I am offended that Otani does not come to see me. He must see my partner. My partner will watch these Shiraishi and Uchibori rats eat each other when I'm gone. Their blood will cleanse the Great Japanese Empire. Then my partner will announce himself to His Majesty, and His Majesty will listen."

Neither Noguchi nor Kimura had been able to get anything further from him, and Otani would himself have dismissed the idea of a secret partner at the head of the

Yamamoto empire as a fiction of a dying, crazy old mind, were it not for Kimura's earnest insistence that Noguchi thought there might just possibly be something in it, and was already mounting a massive informer operation to see what he could glean. So far as Otani was concerned the lack of a clear successor to Yamamoto and the consequent prospect of large-scale gang warfare was bad enough in all conscience.

Many of the flowers in the garden were familiar enough to Otani, though he had never seen such banks and masses of them, or experienced the intensity of the mingled perfumes with which this English sunshine was heavy. As he idly savoured the fragrance and with a part of his mind marvelled at the absence of traffic noise, Otani cast his memory back over occasional rumours which had come to his ears over the years through friends of his in the Kobe South Rotary Club. Very few police officers are accepted into the exclusive ranks of Rotary in Japan, and Otani's welcome into one of the several clubs in Kobe had been to say the least cautious, notwithstanding his impeccable family credentials and local importance.

Mindful of the exceptional honour done to him, Otani comported himself at all times as a minor, insignificant member of the club. However, as the years went by, he, like all the other Rotarians, was increasingly able to turn his membership of a group of a hundred or so influential and knowledgeable men to account. There had been a spectacular case of arson, and a complicated jewellery swindle and a disagreeable blackmailing, all of which had been cleared up mainly because of crucial items of information passed to Otani in the bar at the New Port Hotel, more often than not without the informant's realising how cleverly Otani had drifted into and past the subject.

Whenever he was prevented for some reason from attending the regular weekly lunchtime meeting on Tuesdays at his own club, Otani like other Rotarians was obliged to "make up" his attendance record by visiting some other Rotary Club which met on a different day. This obligation and the unpredictable pattern of his official duties meant that he had visited most of the neighbouring clubs from time to time, including the mighty Osaka Club, second only to the Tokyo Club in exclusiveness.

It was at the Osaka Rotary Club that Otani had once had pointed out to him the famous Mr Murakami, the tycoon who was thought to have more politicians in his pocket than any other businessman in Japan. At that time Otani knew no more about Murakami than any reasonably well-informed citizen. He saw him on television commercials, exhorting assemblies of scrubbed and smiling boys and girls to honour their parents and to take plenty of exercise; Murakami was indeed frequently shown jogging a few metres with them along some leafy lane. The film would then be cut to a dramatic scene at the races, since it was from gambling concessions that Murakami made the bulk of his money.

He knew that Murakami was an extravagant philanthropist, who by means of judicious donations to newsworthy causes had collected a number of medals and honours of one sort and another, not only in Japan but from various international agencies; and he knew him to be a prominent rightist. Nevertheless, Otani had at that time no grounds to suppose that Murakami had any direct links with organised crime, of which he was a passionate and eloquent public enemy, calling in frequent speeches for its ruthless suppression by the forces of law and order.

All the same, this was the man whom he had been asked to keep an unobtrusive eye on.

Otani still thought the security authorities had gone about things in a peculiar way. Given that the Embassy man, Noda, had taken the trouble to go all the way out to Heathrow, he might just as well have told Otani personally that word was out that an attempt might be made on Murakami's life while he was in Britain as one of the benefactors involved in the Nantemo Institute project. Instead he had told Shimizu, who had passed the information on when they arrived at St John's Wood. Otani had no intention of undertaking a low-grade—and unpaid—assignment as a bodyguard, and would in any case have been entirely incompetent to do so, but he realised that he would now in any case keep a professional eye on the proceedings, and was quite looking forward to seeing Murakami again. There was no reason in the world to suppose that if Yamamoto actually had a secret partner it was Murakami, but now that the notion had found lodgement in his head it was proving oddly difficult to get rid of.

"I see that my most honoured guest is admiring my flowers," the Master said in his antique Japanese, suddenly materialising at Otani's elbow. "I fear that you must find the crudity of the display offensive. So many colours all jumbled together. One recalls the tart remarks of the Lady Sei Shonagon in her pillow Book about the unfortunate effect of a clash of hues among the under-robes of a certain Court lady."

Otani looked up at the tall old man with friendly warmth in his heart. "The flowers are beautiful," he said. "Please forgive my inquisitiveness, but did you live for a long time in Japan?"

Sir Benjamin raised his two hands defensively. "I have never visited your country," he said. "My Japanese friends are very kind and urge me to do so, but I fear that I would find it much changed, and perhaps in unwelcome ways."

"Changed?" Otani was baffled, and the Master nodded understandingly.

"I must explain. I fell in love with the idea of your country as a boy, when an old uncle of mine who had been in the Diplomatic Service told me the legends of the gods who created those islands. He taught me a few words of your language, and showed me how to write some of the simpler characters with brush and ink." The Master absent-mindedly sketched a few strokes in the air, then sternly restrained himself. "The old fellow was very upset with me later, though," he went on. "When I decided that the Buddhism he had embraced was not for me, and began to take an interest in Shinto and Court ritual instead. But I wander. I wander. Some other time, perhaps, for there are great things afoot today, are there not? Indeed I fancy that your Ambassador has just arrived . . . forgive me once more, dear sir."

Otani had already noticed that during part of the Master's disquisition a small, anxious man dominated by a voluminous black gown had been trying to attract his attention, and Sir Benjamin now hastened off with him to greet the Japanese Ambassador. Otani then realised that some kind of procession was being formed near a tall wrought-iron gate in the high, mellow-bricked wall of the garden. The gate had been opened to disclose more expanses of lawn, and it was obvious that all the guests were to pass that way.

"Isn't it exciting, and so . . . *traditional?*" It was a gushing Japanese lady speaking, one of the group who had borne Hanae away earlier and who was now restoring her to Otani. "I'm Mrs Kubo," she announced to him in an extraordinary display of forwardness, "and this is my daughter Tomoko."

"Otani," he replied grimly, softening his expression somewhat as he bowed slightly to Tomoko who proved to be a girl of about seventeen. He thought she was quite pretty in spite of a worldly-wise look about her eyes unusual in a Japanese girl of that age. Her Liberty print dress in soft gentle colours was charming too, though he found himself wondering what Hanae was thinking about the low, scooped-out neckline which revealed the beginnings of the cleavage between Tomoko's small breasts.

"Hello," said Tomoko casually. "Sorry, I don't speak much Japanese."

"Tomoko-san goes to school here in Cambridge," Hanae explained hastily. "Za Paasu Sukuuru."

"Perse School, yes," Tomoko agreed, making it sound quite different. "It's not a bad place."

"Tomoko speaks perfect English," Mrs Kubo interrupted smugly. "So does my husband, of course, because of his work on Thomas Hardy, you know. He's, well, they don't use the title Visiting Professor here, but that's what he is, of course. To all intents and purposes."

Otani felt obliged to offer some contribution to the conversation, though his eyes kept straying to the scene near the gate, where the small man in the black gown was darting back and forth in an attempt to prevent his unruly charges from straying out of line. There were at least half a dozen other Englishmen wearing red robes similar to the Master's, and several in black ones with colourful hoods drooping down their backs.

Murakami was there with the other visiting businessmen in their obviously made-in-Japan dark suits, and was at that moment engaged in conversation with Sir Benjamin, who nodded vigorously and pointed back to the open french windows, then made an angular gesture or two at which Murakami nodded too, with what from a distance looked more like relief, and trotted off, quite obviously in the direction of the lavatory.

"Are there many Japanese scholars living here in Cambridge?" he asked, gazing at Murakami's receding back until he disappeared behind a milling group of guests. Nobody else seemed to be paying the least attention to him. Shimizu had told Otani that Murakami had been in particularly good form on arrival in London, though disappointed to learn that the Playboy Club had lost its gambling licence.

"Oh, several," fluted Mrs Kubo. "My husband of

course is the most senior, but then there are three or four young trainee diplomats from our Foreign Ministry . . . charming young men." She beamed archly at Tomoko who turned away with a bored look on her pretty painted face. "Then there's a rather tiresome person, Dr Tawara the physicist. From a minor private university near Kobe, I believe. He's over there somewhere." Mrs Kubo gestured vaguely towards the end of the garden.

It was not the news of Dr Tawara's place of origin which interested Otani so much as the colour which came to Tomoko's cheeks as her mother spoke. "Oh look, I believe they're ready!" There was certainly a sudden flurry of activity among the men at the gate, and Otani saw the commanding figure of Sir Benjamin with the Ambassador at the front, raising his arm in the manner of John Wayne leading the US Cavalry into action.

Then he set forth with a measured tread, brushing off what seemed to be some sort of objection from Otani's son-in-law Akira Shimizu, who looked round rather wildly then fell into place as the procession straggled out of the garden two by two, each English academic with a Japanese partner. As Otani watched, the Japanese Embassy man Noda detached himself and made straight for Otani, who moved away from the women to meet him.

"He went to the toilet," Otani said crisply, and indicated the direction discreetly as he fell in beside Noda, whose eyes were flickering about the garden, now rapidly emptying as the remainder of the Master's guests trailed along in the wake of the formal procession. Noda made no reply, and the two men were soon through the study and in the big vestibule of the Lodge.

The cloakroom set aside for the use of male guests was large, with room to accommodate not only overcoats and belongings in some quantity, but also two wash-hand basins with mirrors above them, and a table on which old-fashioned hair brushes were set out on a white cloth. The

WC cubicles, two of them, were in an inner part, and the door of one was closed.

"Murakami-san!" Noda spoke sharply and distinctly, rapping on the door as he did so. There was no reply, but the door yielded to his hand and swung ajar. Murakami was in no position to protest, sitting as he was fully dressed on the closed lavatory seat, leaning against the corner of the cubicle with one elbow resting almost casually on the toilet roll holder. This was because he was dead.

Otani elbowed Noda aside and edged carefully into the cubicle. Most of the blood had soaked into Murakami's clothes, and the dark suit still looked quite presentable. The jacket was open, though, and the handle of the knife protruding from his chest was clearly visible. Otani saw at once that the crest on it was that of the College, since he had noticed it on the plates of dry biscuits being handed round with the sherry.

Chapter 5

Cambridge

HANAE THOUGHT IT ALL QUITE DELIGHTFUL, AND EVEN trailed her fingers in the chilly water for a few minutes as the punt noiselessly drifted along the Backs. It had been worth facing Mrs Kubo's evident disapproval when Dr Tawara the physicist suggested over lunch that since there was nothing further on the programme until tea, Mrs Otani—and perhaps Miss Kubo—might care to see some of the other beauties of Cambridge from the viewpoint provided by a cushioned seat in a punt; especially as Hanae had received a fascinating letter from her sister that morning.

Tomoko accepted eagerly, and Hanae could herself see why, since Dr Tawara was a decidedly attractive man, in spite or perhaps because of his air of distinguished melancholy. Whatever her feelings, Mrs Kubo could scarcely hope to find a more respectable chaperon for her daughter than Hanae, and she consented with an ill grace to the arrangement.

"What did you enjoy most about the opening ceremony?" enquired Dr Tawara courteously as he repositioned the pole for another pass. He was a man in his late thirties, Hanae judged, with a thick shock of "romance grey" hair, fetchingly tousled as a result of his exertions.

"Oh, everything," she said helplessly. "That lovely old hall with the paintings and the carved wood, and the beautiful robes the English professors were wearing, and, oh, the *surprise* when they unveiled the panel on the wall and the Master read out the *haiku* on it and spoke so elegantly in Japanese."

Tomoko was squirming about ecstatically on the seat beside Hanae and took no part in the conversation, being content to gaze besottedly at Dr Tawara. "Oh yes, the *haiku.* The Master actually composed it himself, you know. His calligraphy is old-fashioned, but quite fine. The poem has seventeen syllables in the English version too:

'Bounty from the East:
Unworthy recipients,
We honour our friends'."

Hanae could not understand the English words, and the sound was not as euphonious as that of the Japanese the Master had intoned to the delight of his foreign guests, though very much more so than the stilted acceptance speech of the leading Japanese representative when he received from Sir Benjamin's hands the original brushwork on hand-made paper, mounted on a silken scroll.

"How nice it must be to study in this splendid place," she said dreamily, recalling the crowded ugly campus of the junior college for women at which she had earnestly studied Japanese literature and the history of art, with supplementary courses in home economics thirty years and more before. It seemed a pity to her that after not only missing the ceremony, her husband had approached her hurriedly as they were all on the way to Hall for lunch, excused himself and gone off again, taking Shimizu with him.

"It's like all universities in many ways, though, in spite of the old buildings, and traditions and space." Dr Tawara paused to dab at his forehead with a paper handkerchief. "Nevertheless there are pressures, arguments, problems. I think you said you have a sister who is a professor?"

"No, no. Not a professor. An *assistant* professor at a private women's university." Though, Hanae reflected, to judge by the airs and graces she affected, her sister might imagine herself to be a senior academic at the legendary Tokyo University itself. "As a matter of fact, I think you may know her. Her name is Michiko Yanagida."

Hanae watched Tawara's face carefully but concluded from his expression that he had made a greater impression on Michiko than she on him. But although Tawara shook his head and his wiry arms seemed tireless as he propelled the punt through the water he did seem to sag a little, and Hanae thought she could see exhaustion and loneliness in the hooded eyes. Tomoko at her side could, it seemed, scarcely keep her hands off him.

"No," Tawara said. "I can't say I recall the name. Which university?"

Hanae decided not to press the point, being more concerned to establish whether or not Dr Tawara was married. She assumed he must be; for otherwise it would be difficult to account for Mrs Kubo's evident distaste for him and anxiety over Tomoko's equally evident infatuation. "It's not important," she said, waving away the question with a smile. "It must be difficult for a Japanese man living alone in another country," she then hazarded, aware as she spoke of the heavy-handedness of her approach.

"I'm lucky," he said tersely. "St Cuthbert's has good accommodation for graduate students, and they allowed me to move into one of the small flats in the same building which they reserve for overseas researchers."

"It's beautiful," Tomoko blurted out, then went crimson with embarrassment and stared fixedly at a tree they were passing. Hanae decided that she had not heard the remark, but Tawara cleared his throat awkwardly.

"I suppose we should be getting back for tea," Hanae said to relieve the tension, looking at her watch. Although she was now more or less adjusted to local time, she felt very sleepy and was wondering if she might encourage Otani to doze off in the car going back to London, so that she could follow suit. She had no idea how far they had come in the punt, but Tawara seemed entirely confident. He nodded and somewhat surprisingly continued in the same direction, but more vigorously.

They disembarked some twenty minutes later, Tomoko seemingly having some difficulty in getting out of the punt. At all events she leant heavily on Tawara and he slipped an arm round her waist as she finally stepped up on the jetty, withdrawing it only when he met Hanae's gaze.

Hanae could have sworn they had travelled a great distance in the punt, but they were now, confusingly, so near to St Cuthbert's again that she could recognise the cathedral-like buildings in which the ceremonies had taken place and lunch had been served by middle-aged women with cheerful red country faces, creakingly corseted within black waitress uniforms. Hanae had noticed them particularly and admired their little white aprons trimmed with broderie Anglaise. Tawara pointed out the direction to the Master's Lodge at which it had been announced that tea would be served to the Japanese visitors, and Hanae thanked and left them. She noticed a few moments later as she rounded a corner that Tomoko was by then openly clutching Tawara's hand, but her musings were interrupted when the gateway to the Lodge came into view.

Having earlier been hospitably open, the high wrought-iron gates with the College crest picked out in gold and red were now firmly closed. Moreover a large policeman in uniform stood outside them, and a small group of onlookers were on the opposite side of the street, talking animatedly among themselves.

Bewildered, Hanae hesitantly approached the policeman. The only alternative would be to hasten back and try to find Tawara and Tomoko, but judging by the way Tomoko had seized his hand the moment she thought Hanae could no longer see them, they would have disappeared long since. Her heart sank as the policeman raised a formidable hand and uttered a sentence which was completely incomprehensible to her; and Hanae stood irresolutely, completely at a loss. The towering officer in the huge helmet spoke again, and Hanae was desperately trying to compose a sentence in English when the great door of the Lodge at the end of the lengthy front garden opened, and Otani, Noda and Shimizu emerged.

Hanae's relief at the sight of them was so great that for a while she quite forgot to wonder what was going on. Otani spotted her at once and all three men hurried to the gate, where Noda spoke to the policeman, opening the small wicket gate at the side as he did so. With some reluctance the big Englishman waved Hanae through and Otani drew her aside. The look of excitement in his eyes told her almost as much as the words he used to give her a brief account of his and Noda's discovery of Murakami's body, of the summoning of the Cambridge police and the hasty decision to allow the ceremony to go forward as arranged without informing the Master or the other guests about what had happened until after lunch.

Otani had sat in with Shimizu while he briefed the visiting Japanese business leaders about the "sudden death" of their colleague along lines agreed after Noda had conferred with his Ambassador, and the Master persuaded the Cambridge police to reveal as little as possible to the Press during the initial stages of enquiries.

All plans had been changed. The Otanis were to stay at the Garden House Hotel overnight instead of returning to

London, while Shimizu escorted his surviving charges there. Noda too would remain in Cambridge, and after checking in at the hotel Noda and Otani were off to police headquarters in Parkside next to the Fire Brigade to prepare their statements.

Mrs Kubo had already got wind of excitements afoot, and Hanae was invited to tea with her at her home. Hanae would on the whole have greatly preferred to wait quietly at the hotel for Otani's return, and therefore smiled all the more brightly at her husband as he told her, while leading the way out and towards a waiting police car. Having only recently left Tomoko clinging to Dr Tawara, Hanae did not relish being closeted with Mrs Kubo, but there was little point in arguing. Otani was capable of rational speech, but not of listening, and Hanae guessed that he had already formed and discarded several theories. He was happy as a lark.

Chapter 6

Kobe

"IT IS MY BELIEF THAT MR BIG IS DEFINITELY MURAKAMI," Kimura said portentously as he and Noguchi descended into the vast underground shopping complex at the busy Sannomiya junction in Kobe. Having decided to assume the role of a journalist, Kimura dressed down for the occasion, in a casual jacket and lightweight slacks. Nevertheless they made an odd pair, since Noguchi was wearing his day-labourer outfit; an old vest, pantaloons somewhat like scruffy jodhpurs, and rubber-soled legging-boots with a separate compartment for the big toe. A purple knitted belly-band protruded above his breeches. Noguchi was, however, carrying a metal tool-box in one gnarled hand, and Kimura hoped and believed that passers-by would take him for a workman being led to the site of a job by his employer.

"Don't think you should go there," was all Noguchi grumbled by way of reply.

"Can't do any harm," Kimura argued airily. "Look how useful our visit to Yamamoto was. Just in time before he died, too. The Chief was delighted when I rang him in London." This time Noguchi managed only a snort as Kimura paused to admire the display in an expensive menswear boutique they were passing.

"Anyway, I can't see why you need to come, especially if you're only going to hang about outside."

"Must keep some sort of an eye on you. Fat chance of them taking me for a reporter." Noguchi's comment prompted Kimura to take a leather card-case from his pocket and check that he had at least three or four of the right ones with him. There had two years before been an unfortunate occasion when, posing as an airconditioner salesman, he had by mistake profferred a card describing himself as a marriage guidance consultant. Had the name on it been different he would have been able to explain it away easily. It is not at all unusual for Japanese to carry about with them the cards of other people they have met, and this is indeed why the madams of expensive bars and managers of high-class restaurants will generally require customers asking for credit to present *two* copies of their name-cards.

Reassured, Kimura pressed on, with Noguchi complaining in his wake, and soon the two men emerged into the open air again having crossed the huge intersection, and made their way towards the north-east quarter of the inner city, where the offices of the Murakami Foundation for peace and Population Control were located.

They both paused on the opposite side of the broad street while still some distance away, and looked diagonally across at the solid, almost bank-like respectability of the façcade. The Murakami building was not very lofty, consisting of only three floors; but it had clearly been built at considerable expense and not so very many years earlier. A short flight of marble steps led up to an imposing main entrance, to one side of which was a massive granite panel with the name of the Foundation incised deeply and impressively in Chinese characters, legible even at that distance.

Noguchi shook his head slowly and let out a philosophic sigh. "Going through with it?" he demanded.

"Of course. You never know." Kimura's tone was nonchalant, but he was nevertheless apprehensive as he waited for a break in the traffic and then jauntily crossed the street in defiance of the strict regulations against jay-walkers. By the time he reached the other side and looked back, Noguchi had already opened up his tool-box and was at work unscrewing the cover of a junction box on an electrical supply pole a few yards along the street, to all intents and purposes invisible to the people passing by.

It seemed pretty clear that Murakami's philanthropic activities hardly called for administrative support of the complexity suggested by the exterior of the building, since the greater part of the ground floor consisted of a huge open lobby which served also as an exhibition area. In the centre was a hideous life-sized bronze statue of a man listening with a kindly expression on his tilted face to what the sculptor evidently intended as a supplication of some kind from a small child of indeterminate race, in rags.

Round the walls were panels of photographs and greatly enlarged copies of certificates, awards and citations of one kind and another. The only other person in sight was an old janitor in a blue uniform, perched on a stool near the entrance and reading the sports page of a cheap newspaper with moody concentration. He did no more than glance at Kimura and point at a sign indicating that the reception desk was on the floor above, but before going up Kimura wandered around looking at the pictures, which were almost without exception of Murakami. Murakami in a white safari suit in what might have been a Thai village, surrounded by grinning locals looking at a spanking new white ambulance. Murakami in a business suit being received in audience by the President of the Philippines. Murakami in baggy shorts pretending to chop firewood among merry Boy Scouts, and many others of the same kind.

A sort of holy of holies had been constructed to one side. This consisted of a panel covered with rich brocade and bearing one photograph only, in a huge gold-lacquer frame. The picture was of Murakami in morning suit, bowing very low before the Emperor of Japan. In front of it was a stand surmounted by a glass case. In the case, on a velvet cushion, were the insignia of the Order of the Chrysanthemum.

In spite of his profession, Kimura remained in many ways a naive and impressionable man. As he mounted the stairs to the second floor he was in a condition of some awe and not at all sure that he would be able to carry off an interview with the great man even if granted one.

The second floor was much more like a conventional, if expensive, office suite. A reception desk was placed so as to intercept the visitor, but was unoccupied. A brushed-aluminium signboard with black lettering was affixed to the wall at one side, and Kimura stepped over to read it. Several apparently separate administrative entities were listed. The Murakami Foundation was certainly one, but there was also the Peace Research Association, the Horse Racing promotion Society, the Fund for Third World Advancement and the Citizens' Awareness Movement.

Arrows beside each title indicated one of the two directions in which it was possible to go, so Kimura decided to head for the office of the Murakami Foundation for Peace and Population, passing the Citizens Awareness Movement on the way. There was nobody about in the corridor, but the door of this organisation's office was ajar, and as he approached, Kimura heard male voices raised in apparent agitation.

The time had clearly come for him to make his presence in the building known to someone in authority so Kimura cleared his throat noisily. The effect was electric, in that a profound silence followed, lasting fully ten seconds before the door was flung wide and a man looked out.

Though well-tailored, he looked tough and potentially menacing. He was perhaps thirty, certainly a good ten years younger than Kimura, and was a much bigger man. He wore his hair cropped short in the style of extreme right-wing political activists, and as he looked Kimura up and down Kimura noticed with a flicker of satisfaction that he was going bald at the crown. Through the wide-open door Kimura could see another, still younger man of broadly similar appearance but with a weak face on which was a look of consternation. and more surprisingly, an extremely good-looking girl wearing a dull green overall outfit of excellent cut but with a military look to it.

"Who are you? What do you want?" The man barked at Kimura in the plainest of language, bereft of any of the usual courtesies.

Kimura decided to be equally curt. "Press," he said, thrusting his bogus name-card at the man. *Kobe Shimbun."* He was about to go on and explain that he was researching an in-depth piece about Japanese attitudes to the North-South dialogue and the problems of over-population, but remained silent when a most satisfactory expression of nervousness appeared on the man's coarse features. He ignored Kimura's card, for which Kimura was later grateful.

"Hell, it must be on the wire services already," snapped the girl, pushing past the second man and coming out into the corridor. Even though Kimura's brain was working fast to adjust to what seemed a potentially interesting situation, he had time to reflect briefly that she reminded him of an erotic novel he had once read about the sex lives of Israeli girl soldiers. Her short curly black hair framed a pair of big intelligent eyes, and although her expression was unfriendly, her mouth was wide and her lips full. They stared at each other for a while, Kimura willing her to speak first.

"Well, what do you expect us to say?" she demanded at last. "It's terrible. You can't have a statement yet. We'll issue one later."

"Came as a complete surprise?" Kimura suggested, not having the least idea what she was talking about, but noting with interest that the big man whom he had taken to be in authority seemed content to defer to her.

"Of course it was a surprise," the girl said witheringly. "What did they say about him on the wire anyway?" There was a hint of suspicion creeping into her voice and a new wariness in the man's eyes that Kimura didn't much care for.

"They didn't go into details," he said with a shrug, hoping for inspiration. "Just the bare announcement."

The girl seemed to decide that she had said enough. "We're not talking to the Press," she said decisively. "If you people don't have a London office you'll have to wait to get it from the papers that do. Look, we're busy now . . ."

"Sure, sure," Kimura said hurriedly. "Sorry. I realise it must have come as a big shock. We shall have to print something, of course, but we have plenty of photos on file." He was as glad to go as the oddly-assorted trio seemed anxious to be rid of him, and on regaining the entrance hall Kimura nodded cheerfully at the old janitor, who continued his morose study of the baseball results.

Kimura crossed the street, more demurely this time, allowed himself a broad wink at Noguchi as he passed, then dawdled outside a bookshop looking through the magazines on the display racks until Noguchi completed his pseudo-work and shuffled by in turn. The two men did not speak to each other until they were a full city block away from the Murakami building.

Then, having judged it safe to do so, Kimura closed up with Noguchi, bursting with his news. "What did I tell you, Ninja! Fantastic! I arrived at just the right moment."

"Serving coffee, were they?" Noguchi's lips hardly seemed to move as he trudged along, and Kimura ignored his remark anyway.

"Something's happened to Murakami: it can only be him. Something to do with London. I got far more out of them than I could have hoped."

"Didn't see him then. Murakami."

Kimura gesticulated as he walked, unheeding of the curious glances of people passing by. "I keep *telling* you, Ninja. Just a minute—and hurry up, we've got some phone calls to make. There was this girl, you see . . ." It was as well that Kimura failed to hear Noguchi groan, but in any case he was soon fairly into a reasonably full and accurate account of his encounter with the two men and the woman, and Noguchi held his peace as they walked on, unconsciously quickening their pace as they neared headquarters. By the time they arrived even Noguchi was betraying a hint of excitement in his manner, and he finally admitted that it seemed difficult to put any other interpretation on the woman's remarks than that some disaster had befallen Murakami or someone close to him, and that the British Press would be likely to publicise it.

It took Noguchi half an hour of careful telephoning to locate a contact who would not only admit to knowing Murakami's private telephone number but who was prepared to divulge it, and it was only after a further twenty minutes of hard argument that he eventually gave his grudging consent to Kimura's plan. This was that he, Kimura, should telephone the Murakami residence, still in the guise of a journalist, this time positively seeking confirmation of rumours about Murakami. As Kimura pointed out, they could lose nothing by this stratagem and might gain valuable time. If Murakami were perhaps dead as well as old Yamamoto, and their working hypothesis about a link between the two men proved to be valid, the game would be wide open.

Although glad to have won his point at last, Kimura was slightly disappointed that Noguchi turned down flat an alternative and, to Kimura, more attractive idea of contacting Murakami's household pretending to be a funeral director or even a Buddhist priest enquiring whether there might be any need for his services.

It worked. Kimura was always good on the phone, and though he had no idea of the identity of the woman who answered when he rang the number supplied to him by Noguchi, it was simplicity itself to elicit from her confirmation of Murakami's death in England, and even to find out that the first news of this had been received late the previous evening, by means of a phone call from Cambridge.

Kimura had of course heard of Cambridge, and recalled having seen a week or two earlier an item about Cambridge University in one of the four English-language newspapers published in Japan, all of which were delivered routinely to his office and which he tried to scan each day for the sake of tit-bits of information they sometimes contained about prominent foreign residents in the Kobe area.

Noguchi had disappeared from Otani's ante-room after listening expressionlessly to the telephone conversation on the extension instrument on the clerk's desk, and Kimura was unable to locate him to share his triumphant satisfaction when his assistant, Detective Patrolman Migishima, traced the news item in question, which mentioned the fact that the Chairman of the Board of the Nantemo Trading Company would be accompanied when he went to England to attend the opening ceremony of the new Institute by a number of other prominent businessmen and public figures.

Although the distinguished Kobe philanthropist Mr Shigeru Murakami was not mentioned by name, this particular part of the jigsaw puzzle seemed to fit very neatly. The question was what to do next, given that Otani was in England and would have views of his own. Kimura was ebullient by nature, but experienced a familiar feeling of momentary deflation as he viewed the likely prospect that the Chief might indeed have intervened already. On the other hand, the girl in the green overalls could prove a useful contact, and seemed to have an unusually good figure for a Japanese.

Chapter 7
Cambridge

HANAE STOLE SEVERAL GLANCES AT HER WRIST-WATCH during the two hours she spent with Mrs Kubo, but this was because she feared she might have to leave before covering all the ground she wanted to, not because she was bored. In fact her mood had changed to one of lively interest as soon as she noticed with satisfaction that the flat was not nearly so luxurious as the one occupied by the Shimizus in London. In the first place it was not in a block, but constututed the upper regions of an old house built of red brick and standing in a big but untidy garden littered with children's playthings. A swing dangled drunkenly from one supporting rope, the other having parted, and there were odds and ends of garden furniture about, some broken and all caked with grime and soiled with bird droppings. The sky had clouded over by the time Hanae had arrived, and the dismal garden looked decidedly depressing.

There were bicyles propped here and there outside the porch, which seemed to be full of rubber boots, umbrellas and old raincoats. Within, the hall was large and the majestic tick of the gandfather clock against one wall made Hanae think of museums. Nevertheless, Mrs Kubo's extravagant expressions of admiration for their rented quarters as the epitome of gracious English-style living struck Hanae as excessive.

The big sitting-room upstairs was interesting, though, if only because of its enormous size and the fact that there was a grand piano in it and an open fire in the grate, in spite of the season. It did not take Hanae long to elicit from Mrs Kubo that her husband, though undoubtedly a teacher in good standing, was far from being the Visiting Professor she had earlier implied. but was employed as an instructor in the Japanese language.

Mrs Kubo puzzled Hanae. She appeared to be in her later thirties, which fitted in with the age of her daughter Tomoko, but she dressed in a style which was much too young for her, and the gushing, patronising way in which she spoke seemed to Hanae oddly incongruous. Mrs Kubo was very proprietorial about England in general and Cambridge in particular as she offered tea with milk and some very heavy cakes which she described to Hanae as "scones", understood to be of Scottish origin. She also talked altogether too much about Tomoko, though to Hanae's relief made no enquiry of her as to the girl's present whereabouts. Motherly concern would have been entirely appropriate in that respect, but in fact Mrs Kubo was more interested in the fact that she and Tomoko could wear each other's clothes and frequently did. Hanae scarcely knew where to look.

Mrs Kubo was obviously proud of capturing Hanae as a new friend despite her earlier coolness when the ride in the punt had been proposed, and now treated her as a distinguished person. Hanae was singularly free from snobbery, but did have a proper sense of what was due to the wife of the chief of the third biggest police force in Japan, after Tokyo and Osaka, with nearly nine thousand men under his command. Moreover she had decided that, whatever Mrs Kubo's background might be, she was vulgar and unsuccessful in her bid to be lady-like. Hanae easily enough fended off a few clumsy attempts on Mrs Kubo's part to discover how much Hanae knew about what happened at the Master's Lodge, but as the minutes ticked away Hanae was more concerned to get round to the subject of Tawara.

"Since arriving in England I've had a letter from my younger sister," Hanae said as she declined with a polite gesture the offer of yet another cup of tea. "It seems that the weather for the Golden Week holidays wasn't at all good in her part of Nara prefecture." On Hanae's lap was an album of photographs which Mrs Kubo had urged her to look at, and which she had been leafing through obediently while they were chatting.

Most of the pictures in which Mrs Kubo herself appeared had been taken with some technical skill, though others which it seemed likely were her own work were quite extraordinarily incompetent. Most of them depicted Tomoko in various outfits: playing tennis, with a group of English girls in Perse School uniform, in Girl Guide uniform when obviously about two years younger, and in a party dress which Hanae reflected uncharitably might well have been borrowed from her mother.

"Oh yes, I believe you mentioned your sister when we first met. A professor, you said. Where is it that she teaches?"

"Until recently she'd been at a junior college in Nara for years, but now she's at Doshisha Women's College in Kyoto, actually," said Hanae modestly, and Mrs Kubo's blueshadowed eyes widened in awe.

"But . . . that's very famous!" Hanae could do no more than pretend to ignore the remark. Her sister's university was indeed one of the most prestigious women's establishments in western Japan, though Hanae privately considered its reputation not to be such as to justify the airs Michiko put on and the pretentious written style she affected.

"It's a small world," Hanae said as off-handedly as she could. "She heard my husband and I were coming to Cambridge and said she was acquainted with Dr Tawara. Isn't that a coincidence?" Mrs Kubo's reaction was entirely satisfactory. Her lips became compressed in a thin line, and a bright spot of colour appeared in each cheek. "My sister is a historian and doesn't know many scientists, of course, but it seems that they were members together of some kind of committee set up a few years ago to advise the Association of Private Universities in Japan on something to do with student loans."

Hanae's sister had indeed written along these lines, but Hanae omitted to add that in an uncharacteristic burst of candour Michiko had also written that she much admired Dr Tawara and had been quite upset when their "friendship"—the word was emphasised in the letter—had been interrupted by his acceptance of the research fellowship at Cambridge. Having refused throughout her marriageable years all suggestions that she should be introduced to eligible potential husbands, it seemed almost unbelievable that Michiko should have apparently lost her head at the age of nearly forty.

Hanae thought that of course Mrs Kubo was about the same age, as her hostess blinked, poked the fire and generally fidgeted while trying to decide what to say. What eventually came out did not altogether surprise Hanae. Mrs Kubo looked at her with an expression in which despair and bewilderment were mingled with some other emotion that Hanae could not read. "I wondered if," she faltered, "that is, my rudeness is unpardonable . . . may I confide in you?" For the first time since she had met Mrs Kubo, Hanae began to like her a little.

"Of course . . . if there is anything I can do to help you . . .

"It's Tomoko. My daughter. I'm afraid that she is . . . having an affair with Tawara *Sensei,*" Mrs Kubo went on, picking with disastrous effect at a loose thread in her unsuitably youthful frilly blouse.

Hanae thought quickly. That much had become perfectly plain to her while she had been in the company of Tomoko and Tawara; and Mrs Kubo's earlier manner on mentioning his name had suggested that she was aware of at least the danger of a relationship or of Tomoko's hesitating on the brink of one.

"Perhaps she may be impressed by him," Hanae said carefully. "It often happens that young girls imagine they may be in love with an older man, but . . ."

"She's sleeping with him. I know it!" Mrs Kubo's voice had taken on a keening quality, as though she were about to become hysterical.

"Are you quite sure?" Hanae felt at the time that it was a stupid question to ask, and moved over to put a comforting hand on Mrs Kubo's shoulder as the other woman gave a kind of snort and began to weep noisily.

It took several minutes for Mrs Kubo to calm down, and as she did what she could to hasten the process, Hanae reflected that all the fuss seemed rather excessive, given that Tawara appeared to be an entirely eligible man apart from the fact that he was obviously at least twenty years older than Tomoko. Her own daughter had without the slightest doubt slept with the man she later married long before there was the smallest prospect of a wedding, and like many another middle-class mother Hanae had lived with the knowledge; not happily, but at least without showy displays of tearful despair.

It was Mrs Kubo herself who volunteered at least a partial explanation when she again became capable of hesitant speech. "He's a bad character, you see. He's a *Communist.* My husband says . . ." Mrs Kubo left the sentence unfinished, and the tears began to flow afresh while Hanae realised that she had not actually met Dr Kubo during the course of the day. To while away the time as Mrs Kubo dried her eyes again, she asked delicately about his whereabouts.

Hanae's question had an electrifying effect on Mrs Kubo, whose expression of misery was at once replaced by one of animal terror. "He was in the garden all the time," she began to babble. "If your husband has been asking questions, well, I absolutely guarantee that he never left the garden. Besides, it's ridiculous to think that Kenji could possibly be involved in such a thing . . ." Mrs Kubo sucked in a great sobbing breath as Hanae gaped at her in amazement.

"I don't understand what you're talking about," she said simply, then impulsively seized Mrs Kubo's hand. "You don't imagine for a moment that I was implying that your husband might have had anything to do with this . . . *murder*, do you?"

Mrs Kubo's make-up was by then completely ruined, but it was not that which made her look ten years older. Hanae was honestly distressed by the haunted look in the other woman's eyes as she began to speak in a low but at last controlled voice. "Pay no attention to what I said. I'm just upset about Tomoko, and . . . my husband's health. He's been acting strangely for months, and won't talk to me. He won't answer any of my questions and gets angry when I persist. He says Dr Tawara is a bad character but he spends a lot of time with him."

"Does he know about your . . . anxiety . . . over Tomoko-san?"

Mrs Kubo nodded her head fiercely. "Yes. He gets insanely furious whenever she and Dr Tawara are even in the same room together. I was so frightened that he would make a scene when you wanted to go on the punt this afternoon. But he was out of earshot."

Hanae was utterly at a loss, and had no idea what to say

or do next. She was relieved when the telephone rang and Mrs Kubo went out onto the landing to answer it. While she waited for her to return Hanae looked again through the photograph album, studying particularly the pictures in which Dr Kenji Kubo appeared. He seemed an ordinary enough man, and the fact that he had an earnest, solemn expression on his bespectacled face whether dressed in a formal business suit or in sports shirt and shorts was not in itself remarkable to her.

"It was Tomoko," Mrs Kubo said as she came back into the room. "She's at the Overseas Students' Club with some of her friends. I could hear the noise in the coffee bar there." Her evident relief was pathetic.

"I shall have to go soon," Hanae said, feeling helpless. She had been told that Otani would be brought to pick her up after his session with the Cambridge police, and it was already twenty minutes after the appointed time. "I don't know what I can do to help you, but I think that if you are really worried about your husband, you ought to talk to someone . . . Perhaps the Master of the College? He seems very sympathetic."

Mrs Kubo shook her head heavily. "I was foolish to say so much to you. I have no right to bother you with my problems . . . when you asked me where my husband was, I lost my head. He's teaching this evening, at the Further Education College. Elementary Japanese writing." She forced a smile. All the pomposity had gone from her, all the effusiveness and all the bright social manner of earlier in the day. The doorbell rang, and Mrs Kubo went over to the big window and drew the curtain aside to look out. "It's a police car," she said flatly. "Your husband has come for you."

As they bowed their farewells, Hanae saw before her a frightened, lonely woman, in an agony of uncertainty about some dark side to the man she was married to, and even entertaining nightmare fears that he might that day have committed murder. If that were not enough, her teenage daughter was deeply involved with a man said to have a dubious background, a man old enough to be her father. Undoubtedly an extremely attractive man, though, and it occurred to Hanae that Mrs Kubo might even conceivably be jealous of the daughter whose youth and freshness she strove so hard to preserve in herself. Funnier things had happened.

Chapter 8

London

"OHIO," SAID CHIEF SUPERINTENDENT FRED Nickleby with a broad smile as he wrapped a beefy hand round Otani's and shook it heartily. "I remember a bit of me Japanese, you see," he added to Noda who was standing to one side of Otani.

"Ah," Noda said after a moment's perplexity. "*Ohayo*, of course." He whispered a hurried explanation to Otani that the Chief Superintendent had courteously greeted him in Japanese.

"Ohio. Dowmow. Um . . . let's see, something like obligato . . .

"*Arigato*," Noda contributed helpfully. "Means 'thank you'. *Domo*—much the same thing."

Otani stood nervously smiling as Nickleby exhausted his stock of Japanese, then fingered his tie self-consciously. "Well I'm blowed," Nickleby said with an air of benign astonishment. "Still got the old tie then, have you? Dear oh dear, that takes me back a bit. What was it? Must be seven or eight years ago. Good idea, Interpol holding that study meeting there. Well, nice of you to look me up, Super."

As a matter of fact Nickleby had not the slightest recollection of having met Otani at the conference. He had distributed half a dozen Metropolitan Police Operatic Society ties to Japanese police officers at the farewell buffet reception and was amazed that over the years as many as four of them had now, as it were, come to roost. He surreptitiously peeped at the name card which had been sent in from the reception desk, as he waved Otani and Noda to chairs in the tiny room used for occasional visitors.

"Otani. Remember you well," he lied. "Enjoying old England, then, are you? Sorry I couldn't get out to Heathrow to meet you." Nickleby sat back as Noda interpreted for Otani, allowing him to infer that it was because of the impact of their meeting in Kyoto years before that Nickleby had arranged for the young police inspector to greet the Otanis on their arrival. Nothing would in fact have been further from Nickleby's mind had it not been for some extremely delicate negotiations between Noda and the diplomatic liaison officer of the Special Branch which had taken place within hours of Otani's having submitted his formal application for leave of absence to the Governor of Hyogo prefecture, copy to the National police Agency, Tokyo.

Otani was determined not to neglect the courtesies on this his first visit to Scotland Yard, even though Noda had briefed him carefully on the way about the line to take concerning their discovery of Murakami's body. He therefore embarked on a flowery prepared speech emphasising his sense of privilege in being given this opportunity to visit a place famous throughout the world as the cathedral of police work, and his embarrassment in intruding into Chief Superintendent Nickleby's no doubt breathlessly busy official round. He then unwrapped a silk *furoshiki* square to reveal an opulently packaged bottle of Suntory Royal whisky which he presented to Nickleby with a flourish.

Nickleby appeared to pay no attention to Noda's translation, which was brutally short anyway, and stared thoughtfully at the gift until a young man with a rebellious look on his face brought in a tray on which were three thick white china mugs of pungently strong tea, and a plate of biscuits. "Ah, the cup that cheers but not inebriates," Nickleby remarked with an air of relief as he took one for himself. "Dowmow. Um . . . not sure what to do about this, Super. Very nice of you, I'm sure. Drop of the good stuff by the look of it . . ."

Otani could guess what was passing through his mind. "Tell him it's just a small souvenir. Like this tie he gave me," Otani suggested cunningly to Noda, and Noda did so.

Nickleby brightened, and placed the boxed bottle carefully to one side. "Regulations? Blow that. Very acceptable gift from an old friend and colleague. Go down proper grateful, that will."

He urged his Japanese guests to help themselves to tea. "Sugar? I shall have to use one of these bloody tablets, pardon my French." Otani was perfectly familiar with what the Japanese refer to as *mirukuti* or "milk-tea", though he had seldom drunk it so strong. To be on the safe side he dumped two good heaped spoonfuls of sugar into his while Nickleby shook a sweetener tablet into his own mug from a plastic container he produced from his pocket.

"Well then," Nickleby went on cosily as soon as they had all taken a tentative sip and Otani had been persuaded to try a Chocolate Wholemeal biscuit. "Bit of a busman's holiday, then. Can't keep away from it, can you?" The smile on the rubicund face struck Otani as containing an element of hostility, and he turned to Noda in some curiosity to await an interpretation.

"The Chief Superintendent is bringing up the question of the murder. He's none too pleased about your being involved. I warned you what to expect." Noda sustained a convincing expression of cheery goodwill as he explained, and Otani followed suit.

"Tell him that it was of course pure chance that we came upon the body first. All the same, you had warned the authorities here that there would be considerations of personal security involved with the Japanese VIPs at Cambridge, hadn't you? Otani nodded and smiled at the Englishman as he took another bite of the delicious biscuit.

"Superintendent Otani wants you to know that he doesn't make a habit of this kind of thing, sir," Noda said. "The only reason he and his wife came to England was for a holiday and to see their married daughter and grandson."

"Good lady none too pleased, then, I should reckon. Ah well, bit of excitement at least. Nothing much else until the Trooping of the Colour." Nickleby pulled himself up and hastily assumed a solemn official manner. "Pardon my frivolity, Mr Noda. No offence intended. Very nasty business, very nasty indeed. Important Japanese gentleman like that. As you know, as soon as we got word from the Cambridge force and they asked for our help, we notified your consular people. Very grateful for your on-the-spot assistance, my word, yes."

"No offence taken, Chief Superintendent," Noda said calmly, scrutinising the glowing tip of the cigarette he was as usual holding by the other extremity. "We for our part are very grateful for the discretion shown by the media over this. I'm sure you and the Cambridge police had a hand in that." Privately he imagined that the minimal and carefully worded press publicity had more to do with some discreet pressure applied in the right quarters following a conversation he himself had had with his principal contact in the Foreign Office Security Department. Noda summarised the exchange for Otani, who now sat quietly watching Nickleby's face. He had managed to finish the tea and was surreptitiously removing odd tea-leaves from his teeth, finding time to wonder whether Scotland Yard had ever heard of strainers.

Nickleby was a big, heavy man who in some odd respects reminded Otani of Ninja Noguchi. He was dressed in a perfectly respectable suit and what was left of his hair was neatly combed. Nevertheless, it was clear to Otani that he was a hard man, and probably resourceful. It was tiresome not to be able to understand anything whatever of what was said, but as on a number of previous occasions of the same kind he occupied the time quite profitably by developing his impressions of the characters who were doing the talking, through observation of their facial movements, gestures and intonation.

Otani was beginning to like Noda quite a lot. The man had a chip on his shoulder, no doubt because his upbringing had made him alien to his own people while clearly he could not identify fully with the British. Otani seldom pondered about the characteristics of Japanese society, but something in his nature gave him an instinctive sympathy with misfits. He knew well enough that the outward signs of general conformism concealed many people at odds with life in Japan, even though those who came to his official attention were usually human wrecks, sodden with cheap *shochu* potato spirit, passing their days and nights disregarded in odd corners of railway stations and subways.

Otani's own father had in his very different way been an odd man out: the famous and distinguished professor of chemistry who with a handful of other leading academics stood out with lonely bravery against the hateful activities of the "thought police" of the thirties and was ostracised and reviled for it. Noda didn't need this kind of bravery. As a member of the Japanese diplomatic service he was entrenched in a privileged and élite profession, and his unusual linguistic skills would mean that he would be likely to spend most of his time in Britain or some other English-speaking country. However Otani surmised that he had much to contend with from colleagues who had come up by the conventional route, and that it might be by no means easy for him at times to accept and to support the official Japanese government line.

Once or twice during the ensuing conversation between himself and Nickleby, Noda attempted to summarise it in Japanese for Otani's benefit, but after a while he became too absorbed to do so. It was in fact Nickleby who brought him back into play. "Well, here we are gassing away like a couple of old women leaving our friend here sitting about like a pork chop at a Jew's wedding. Now then, Super, what do you say? Care to give us a bit of a hand, would you?"

The question was clearly addressed to him and Otani turned expectantly to Noda, who nodded almost imperceptibly. "I'll fill you in later." he said to Otani in Japanese. "I think I've managed to persuade him that it's to the advantage of the British police to have you here at this time. Quite apart from the fact that you are a material witness, of course. Would you agree to act as a kind of consultant for a few days? The Embassy would naturally clear it with the National Police Agency and the Governor of Hyogo."

It took Otani no time at all to make up his mind. "Please tell Chief Superintendent Nickleby that I shall be greatly honoured to make myself available to him in any capacity which might be of assistance." Nickleby nodded ponderously while Noda interpreted into English, then stuck out a hand to Otani, who suffered his own to be vigorously shaken for rather a long time.

"Very good of you. Don't mind telling you, I never thought I'd live to see the day I'd be working alongside a Jap copper, but there you are. Right then. Get your computer-assisted skates on, Super. It's back to Cambridge for you, my lad."

Otani heard the offensive word "Jap" clearly enough, and saw Noda wince as the big Englishman used it; but the spirit in which Nickleby had spoken was obviously warm and good-humoured, and all three men stood up for a round of farewells. Nickleby solicitously adjusted Otani's tie for him, winked and patted him on the shoulder as he opened the door, and to his own surprise Otani found that he did not cringe from what would normally have been unwelcome physical contact.

"I shall do my best to be of assistance. Please show your favour to me. We have greatly disturbed you at a busy time." As he uttered them, the everyday conventional Japanese phrases which went largely unheard at home sounded to Otani false and ridiculous and he was relieved when Noda made no attempt to put them into English.

"Cheers, then! All the best," was what Nickleby boomed after them when all three had made their way to the end of the corridor and the lift doors were closing on the two Japanese.

Noda's thin, sardonic face was expressionless until they were out of the building and had almost reached Victoria Street. Then he grinned broadly at Otani. "Well, quite an experience," he said. "What about a beer? How would you like to visit an English pub?"

Otani nodded at once. "Good idea. I want you to fill me in on everything that was said, anyway."

It was only just after twelve noon, and although there was plenty of activity in Victoria Street itself in the mild May sunshine, the pub was still comparatively quiet, with only two or three customers standing at the bar and none sitting at the small tables in what Noda told Otani was called the saloon. Otani sniffed the beery air cautiously, then allowed himself to be led by Noda to the food counter. After one look at the display of sausages, Scotch eggs, veal and ham pies and cold chicken on view, and mindful of the chocolate biscuit he had lately eaten, he opted for a sandwich.

Noda brought them each a pint of beer in a glass mug,

and they silently toasted each other. Within minutes of their arrival the pub had begun to fill up, and Otani was amazed to see the number of women among the customers, but above all, the way in which so many of them came in with male companions rather than in little single-sex groups in the manner of the "office ladies" of Japan. "Different, isn't it?" Noda suggested, correctly interpreting Otani's expression. It was indeed. Otani wanted very much to simply sit there and savour the atmosphere, but forced himself to concentrate on the matter in hand.

"I don't really see how I can help," he said frankly. "I can't understand a word of English, and I don't see what the Chief Superintendent wants of me. Of course, I'll be glad to do anything I can," he added hastily, suddenly fearful that Noda might take him at his word and call the whole thing off.

Noda gulped down a huge amount of his beer and then put the mug down decisively. "Now that we've seen Nickleby I must be more honest with you than I dared to be sooner," he said, glancing around. His voice was low and it seemed extremely unlikely that either the young girl who had joined them at their table or the pimply, clerkly youth with her, who appeared to be an aspiring boy friend, would be able to understand rapid colloquial Japanese. "I'm not a regular diplomat. I work for the Public Security Investigation Agency. Some of us are seconded to the Diplomatic Service to take care of security at our embassies in various countries."

Otani nodded slowly. It was by no means the first time he had come across a member of the PSIA. When he did so in Japan it usually led to one of his rare explosions of royal anger at being as he saw it deliberately excluded from access to information which might have made his job much more straightforward. Indeed, after one such episode the Director of the Agency had felt obliged not only to call on Otani at home to express his apologies and appreciation of his services, but even to hint at offering Otani a senior appointment in the organisation. Nothing had come of it, but Otani had no regrets on that score.

The pale young man had nervously seized the girl's hand and was pumping it spasmodically while she sipped at what Noda told Otani later was a lager and lime. "Of course, the PSIA in Tokyo liaises not only with the police agency but also with the Foreign Ministry."

Otani nodded again. He knew that perfectly well. They *say* they do," he said ruefully. "I see very little evidence of liaison with the police in my part of Japan, though. What's all this leading up to?" Otani had finished his beer and wanted more, so he automatically looked round for a waiter or waitress.

"You have to serve yourself in English pubs," Noda said pointedly. "People take it in turns to buy drinks."

Otani quickly took out his wallet and selected one of the five-pound notes Hanae had acquired from the bank in Osaka before they left. "Is this enough?" Although he urged Noda to buy the drinks on his behalf, Noda smilingly shook his head and insisted that Otani should brave the crowded counter, schooling him in what to say.

It seemed a long time to Otani before he caught the eye of one of the barmen, a lanky fellow with bright red hair, and desperately tried to remember his line as the man took the two empty glass mugs from him.

"Tsu pintsu obu . . ."

"JC, wonnit?" the barman interrupted him cheerfully, and Otani nodded wildly and uncomprehendingly. It was no easy matter to get back to Noda carrying two full mugs of John Courage bitter and a fistful of change, but he managed it and sat down in triumphant relief.

"I hope it's the right kind," he said to Noda. Otani now felt quite light-headed, and by the time he was halfway through the second pint he realised also that the beer was much stronger than the lager he occasionally drank with

Kimura in Kobe. By this time too he had acquired some interesting information from Noda. Systematically but economically, in the expert style of a man experienced in briefing techniques, Noda told a story which fascinated Otani.

He began by explaining that the Public Security Investigation Agency had for many years kept Murakami under observation, mainly on account of his dealings outside Japan. They had amassed substantial evidence to suggest that his various philanthropic projects masked active and complex relationships with extreme right-wing groups in a number of countries which could have serious implications for official Japanese interests.

It seemed that the so-called Red Army faction of left-wing terrorists had got wind of part of the story, and that the Agency in Tokyo had some reason to suppose that Murakami had been singled out as an assassination target. Murakami rarely travelled in Europe, and indeed his overseas trips elsewhere were generally undertaken on his own account and in the company and under the protection of his own henchmen and bodyguards. The visit to England as a member of a high-powered and otherwise entirely respectable delegation of senior businessmen provided, according to information received, an unusual opportunity to get at Murakami. Subsequent events testified to the accuracy of the information, if to nothing else as yet.

"As soon as your own travel plans were reported in the routine way to the National Police Agency, our liaison group with them thought it was almost too good to be true. If anything did happen to Murakami in England we'd have one of the most distinguished and famous police detectives in Japan to collaborate with the British police."

Otani shifted in his seat. He rather regretted the second pint of beer, especially as he was not only feeling slightly fuddled but was also longing to go to the lavatory. "It sounds almost as though you were rather hoping that Murakami *would* be killed," he said.

Noda looked at him blandly. "We won't be sending any flowers to the funeral," he conceded, then with another apparently telepathic moment of insight, "the men's room is through that door."

When Otani returned Noda was standing up, and he led the way out of the pub. "I shouldn't have said all that in there," he remarked as they ambled along the pavement in the direction of Westminster Cathedral. The fresh air cleared Otani's head almost at once. "Where do I come in?" he asked. "Are you asking me to be a party to some kind of deception or coverup? I won't do it, you know."

Noda shook his head. "Absolutely not. You will be associated with a perfectly above-board investigation. The British police will insist on solving this murder and we hope you will do everything in your power to help them. Don't worry, you probably wouldn't have to appear at the trial-we'd try to get the authorities here to agree that your written statement could be put in evidence. We all want to know who killed Murakami. The only confusion which might arise will be due to the fact that before you arrived, we let it be thought by the British that it was *your* life which might be in danger, not Murakami's."

Otani stopped short, thunderstruck. "*Me?* What on earth are you talking about?"

Noda looked at him quizzically. "Is that so unthinkable? I told them—the British Special Branch, my Ambassador, everybody I spoke to—I told them a fairy tale about a gangster vendetta. Basically, I just wanted to draw official attention to you. It was easy to get you invited to the ceremony at Cambridge."

"I shall want to go into all this very thoroughly with you before long," Otani said grimly. "Right now, though, I want to know what passed between you and Nickleby this morning. Oh, and by the way I want to know why all his staff address him as 'Guv'nor'. Now listen to me for a moment. Murakami was murdered in a particularly conspicuous way . . . almost as if whoever was responsible wanted maximum publicity, and the police here must be asking themselves why. Have you been feeding them some kind of story?"

"Not yet," Noda said. "Look, this may take some time. Let's go and sit in the Catholic cathedral and I'll explain. You have to pay to get into most of Westminster Abbey these days.

Chapter 9

Kobe

THE FUNERAL SERVICE FOR KONNOSUKE YAMAMOTO WAS by any reckoning an extraordinary affair; and even though Noguchi had thoroughly disapproved of Kimura's idea of not only borrowing a police helicopter belonging to the neighbouring Osaka force to survey the approaches to the Yamamoto house on the previous day, but actually joyriding in it himself, there could be no doubt that the photographs which had resulted proved to be very useful to the officer commanding the riot police who had been deployed to maintain public order if need be.

In fact, this was the second of two funeral services. The first, the respectable one, had taken place two days earlier in a public hall in Osaka where Yamamoto's office was located, and attracted some hundreds of those of his associates who were in more or less orthodox business, as well as a sprinkling of public officials, one or two national politicians and several television personalities.

"This is the real show of strength," Kimura said to Migishima as they showed their passes to the senior man among a group of helmeted, uniformed police armed with metal shields and long night-sticks who had sealed off the approach road they were using. It was not surprising that the man gave the pair of them an incredulous look before waving them through.

Kimura personally considered that his outfit was a masterpiece. His hair had been cut short, and he had fastened to his upper lip with spirit gum a small, sinister moustache. He was wearing a flashily-cut polyester suit in black and silver zebra stripes, and a pink and white striped shirt with a silver tie, the latter secured with a pearl stick-pin. His cuff-links were of coral. On his feet he wore light grey winkle-picker shoes which caused him some discomfort, and on his little finger a heavy gold and coral ring. His bright eyes lurked behind mirror sunglasses.

Bizarre as his appearance was, it was certainly no more extreme than that of many of the other men who were streaming up the narrow street in the direction of the Yamamoto house. Migishima made an entirely credible *yakuza* subordinate, his beefy frame encased in a much cheaper and plainer suit, but one bought from the same shop as Kimura's, and having the same characteristic cut. At Kimura's insistence Migishima had not shaved that morning, and a trace of stubble did wonders to convey an undertone of thuggishness to his normally naively good-natured features.

"Inspector Noguchi reckons that there are over 450 groups throughout Japan either supervised by Yamamoto's central organisation or maintaining some kind of affiliation," said Kimura, peering down at the small gold-plated badge he wore in his lapel. "He gave me this badge himself. It belongs to a small protection racket outfit in Morioka way up north."

He paused and looked back to where a group of three men were submitting with an ill grace to being frisked by one of the police officers at the barrier. "I heard that you've deployed eight hundred men this morning, sir.'' Migishima's tone was as nearly amused as he dared to make it.

Kimura nodded proudly. ''Quite right, Migishima. Eight hundred, plus fifty riot police with two water-cannon and tear-gas grenades in reserve.''

He looked up quizzically at the much taller young man. ''You sound as if you think that excessive. Well, it isn't. We expect getting on for two thousand gangsters here from all over the country. All the regional bosses have been warned to pass the word along to leave weapons behind, but we shall pick up a good few handguns and knives all the same, you mark my words. Look!'' There was a flurry of action at the barrier as one policeman set his shield down and pinioned the arms of a man from whose inside pocket the searcher had just produced a revolver.

His two associates protested angrily and noisily as their companion was frogmarched away, but were shoved unceremoniously to one side and after a few moments gave up, evidently writing him off. They must already themselves have been searched because they were now on the inside of the checkpoint and began to make their way towards Kimura and Migishima, turning back from time to time to shout a few sullen insults at the police.

Kimura himself moved on, resuming his loftily explanatory tone. ''We have checkpoints at the main stations and at the motorway exits from Nagoya; and the Osaka police are checking arrivals at the airport.''

''A show of strength, you said, sir,'' Migishima prompted him.

''Yes indeed. No need to trouble yourself with the strategic policy considerations, Migishima, but take it from me, this is one occasion where the main contenders for supreme control of the Yamamoto organization will have to show themselves, and in force.''

''Do you think there will be any violence, sir?''

Kimura shook his head. They had come to a point where

the street was becoming crowded, and he lowered his voice. "Not here, no. And probably not today. There'll be some scuffles, I expect. The shoot-out will be in the future, unless we can prevent it."

What few shops there were in the street were closed and shuttered, but there was little if any atmosphere of menace as the pairs and groups of men became compressed into a steady stream moving purposefully towards the house, which was now no more than two or three hundred metres ahead.

In fact the local residents seemed to be treating it almost as a festive occasion, with people leaning out of upper windows to watch the scene below. One enterprising householder had apparently rented the use of an upper room to a television crew from one of the national commercial networks, while nearer the house, Kimura and Migishima passed a foreign news cameraman filming quite unmolested from the top of a lightweight metal step-ladder. One or two of the gangsters smirked self-consciously at the camera as they went by, and Kimura heard some of them call out greetings in fractured English. "Herro! Goodo Morningu!" It began to catch on and Kimura was briefly tempted to join in, but restrained himself sternly and merely scowled at the foreigner and his assistant, a bearded youth who was steadying the foot of the ladder while eating a chocolate bar.

In the immediate neighbourhood of the house all exterior walls were covered to a height of about two metres with perpendicularly striped black and white mourning drapes, and soon the display of wreaths came into view, many of them still in the protective transparent plastic wrappings in which they had been delivered by the florists. Almost without exception they were huge and vulgar, with streamer ribbons inscribed in bold black Chinese characters suspended from them. The inscriptions were mostly names of organisations, with here and there that of an individual. It was impossible to memorise more than a few, and Kimura found himself hoping that the high-resolution camera in the police helicopter which circled continuously overhead was able to shoot from such an angle as to make the writing legible when the pictures were examined in the laboratory at headquarters the following day.

The steady hum of conversation all around died down as they came within fifty metres of the house, where another barrier had been established, this time in the form of a long trestle table manned by at least a dozen hard-eyed men in formal black mourning suits. Fine white cloths covered the tables, and on them had been placed a number of massive black lacquer trays, almost as deep as small suitcases. There were also several open condolence books with ink blocks and brushes, as well as fibre-tipped pens for the use of those who were unhandy at calligraphy.

None of the mourners had come unaccompanied, and though there were a number of pairs like Kimura and Migishima, most were in groups of three or four or sometimes more, and only the senior man in each signed the book and handed over a plump white ceremonial envelope of fine hand-made paper, fastened with braided black and silver cords. The subordinates merely proffered their name-cards only, and were permitted to follow their leader into the forecourt of the house.

When they had discussed the matter at a full-scale staff meeting in Otani's office on the previous day, Noguchi and Kimura had agreed that it was probable that the monetary donations which would be offered at the funeral ceremony would quite possibly amount to as much as 200 million yen, equivalent to a million US dollars, and had speculated about the security arrangements that Yamamoto's former personal retainers would make to deal with such a large sum in cash.

A crack team of armed investigators had searched the house the previous day on the strength of a warrant granted with some reluctance by the District Prosecutor, ostensibly on suspicion of income-tax offences. They had found and confiscated eight guns, two Japanese swords and a number of knives, but there had been no sign of a safe or indeed of significant sums of money.

Kimura and Migishima had now arrived at the tables, and Migishima stood back while Kimura signed himself in as Yukio Imai from Morioka and handed over an envelope containing 100,000 yen in crudely forged notes seized from a Chinese counterfeiter in Kobe the previous month. He knew quite well that what he was doing was not only dangerous but also illegal, but Kimura was temperamentally rash and had a far from tender conscience. In any case, so far as they had been able to learn from the National Police Agency Computer Centre there was no hoodlum called Imai in Morioka, nor a Yutaka Mizuta, which was the name printed on the card which Migishima deposited in one of the lacquer trays.

The custodians of the condolence books and offertory trays in any case paid no attention to what was being written in the books or on the envelopes, being concerned to scrutinise new arrivals for familiar and high-ranking faces. The arrival from a provincial town of a petty baron such as Kimura had been at pains to make himself appear to be was of no account.

The huge iron gates to the house were fully open, and the forecourt was divided by movable bamboo barriers in such a way as to provide two routes, one for arriving and the other for departing visitors. Inside, the lobby was covered with temporary carpeting so that there was no need to take off shoes, and Kimura and Migishima flowed in with the tide. It was difficult for Kimura to recognise the rooms he had passed through a few days earlier on the way with Noguchi to call on the dying Yamamoto, since some partitions had been removed and all the walls were draped with white silk; but before long they came to the central focus of the ceremony.

This was a huge photograph of the late Yamamoto, looking rather more like a dessicated university president or Nobel prizewinner than the most influential single criminal in the history of post-war Japan, such was the look of virtuous disapproval captured by the photographer. The portrait was in a heavy black lacquer frame adorned with black silk ribbons, and was propped on a kind of altar surrounded by banked wreaths of white flowers.

Confident as he was of his disguise, Kimura nevertheless experienced a flutter of sick nervousness as he approached the centrepiece, bowed, and ostentatiously meditated for a few seconds. The gang boss Shiraishi and the doctor Shinobe whom he had met on his former visit were both among the group of men in formal dress who were positioned on the far side of the altar, bowing perfunctorily as each visitor turned to leave; and another person in the background whom he had certainly not dreamed of encountering again in such circumstances.

It was gloomy in the enclosed, shrine-like space, and a good many of the mourners who sported dark glasses like Kimura's had taken them off on entering. On the other hand enough kept them on for Kimura to be able to do so without making himself conspicuous. Fortunately it was not necessary to say anything, and even though Kimura thought he discerned a momentarily puzzled expression drift across Dr Shinobe's otherwise listless eyes he emerged from the house well pleased with his performance as well as profoundly intrigued by what he had seen.

Getting away was rather more difficult than arriving, because as soon as they had gone some distance from the house the little knots of gangsters seemed to become seized by even more of a holiday mood, and were beginning to coalesce into larger assemblies of allies, stopping here and there to stand about talking and eyeing others.

Kimura estimated that he and Migishima had arrived about midway through the proceedings, and it was still possible for them to make their way with only occasional hold-ups to the police checkpoint on the other side from the one by which they had gone to the house. They came near to being accosted by one group but, fortunately, attention was diverted at the crucial moment by yet another TV camera crew.

Control was much looser in the case of departing mourners and Kimura and Migishima slipped through unobtrusively, then moved between two dull grey-painted riot police vehicles: an armoured truck with a water-cannon mounted on the top, and a control van into which Kimura hastily clambered after a quick look round to check that they were not observed.

Ninja Noguchi was inside, to Kimura's surprise wearing drab coveralls of the same type as the officer commanding the riot police detachment who saluted smartly from his sitting position near the radio operator. "Well," said Kimura with great satisfaction as he seized one end of his moustache to pull it off, then winced as he hurt himself. "It was worth it, Ninja." He quickly peeled off his jacket, tie and shirt, and put on a clean white shirt before slipping off the too-tight shoes and the trousers of his dreadful suit.

The riot police officer had turned to attend to a message crackling over the radio, and only Ninja Noguchi watched impassively as Kimura changed into the uniform which had prompted him to such derision not many days earlier; but one corner of his lips twitched as Kimura folded his *yakuza* finery with immense care before stowing it away in the Adidas holdall which had contained the uniform.

"Want some coffee?" Noguchi's tone was unexpectedly friendly, and Kimura glanced at him with a suspicion which was at once stilled as he realised with a quick surge of pleasure that Noguchi was actually pleased to see him back safe and sound.

He nodded and took the proffered plastic up, then called through the open door of the van to Migishima, who was still outside talking to one of his uniformed colleagues. "Migishima! Well done! You're off duty till tomorrow. Don't forget the meeting."

Then Kimura sank gratefully into a folding canvas chair and took a welcome mouthful of the heavily sweetened instant coffee Noguchi had poured from a big vacuum flask. "Going to be trouble, do you reckon?" It was rare for Noguchi to ask anyone's opinion, least of all Kimura's, and he pondered before replying.

"Could be," he said at last. "They're beginning to form up into rival groups. I very much doubt if there are many guns still on them, though, so it'll probably only be punch-ups if they do get going." He gestured towards the water-cannon truck parked alongside. "A squirt or two from that should send them off home quietly." Kimura's legs all at once felt like lead, and though he remained in a good humour he was extremely tired. For the first time he rather wished that Otani had been there to take command.

"What I found out was important. though, Ninja, from the way the chief mourners were lined up inside the house. All the eight "presidium" members were there of course, but the succession is between our friend Shiraishi, and Uchibori from Hiroshima. They were in the principal positions, closest to the altar. It's a good job you made me study those photos. Another thing. There was only one woman in the entire show. Yamamoto's wife died years ago, of course. It was the girl I saw at Murakami's office." He smiled to himself. "She looks terrific in a black kimono."

Chapter 10

Cambridge

THE MASTER OF ST CUTHBERT'S COLLEGE SIGHED happily as the door closed behind Noda and Detective Sergeant Farrier of the Cambridge police. "Now I feel that we may have a proper talk," he said in his old-fashioned, quaintly mannered Japanese. "Farrier. An occupational name, my dear Superintendent. Derived through the Old French from the Latin *ferrus*. One who shoes horses. Now you, sir, like so many Japanese, take your name from the topographical characteristics of the region in which your forebears lived. Otani. Great Valley. Interesting. To me the notion conveys theological, or perhaps one should say eschatological overtones. My own name is, alas, bereft of all but geographical significance."

Otani was wary but content as the old gentleman rambled on. Sir Benjamin was not very different from a good many of the elderly professors who had been his father's friends in the last decade or so of his life, and now that the conversation could take place wholly in Japanese Otani was in no mood to rush it. Although it had only been four days since his first visit to Cambridge, it was pleasant to be back. The visit to Scotland Yard had been fascinating to Otani, and he had derived a certain pleasure from sitting with Hanae, Akiko and his grandson Kazuo on the top of a red London bus for a sightseeing tour of famous places which had previously to him been nothing but brand-names in Japan. Trailing round the shops was no fun at all, though, especially as he had been fretting to involve himself in the investigations in Cambridge.

He had travelled to Cambridge by train that morning with Hanae and Noda and enjoyed the ride, though conversation had been difficult, since Otani had promised Hanae that he would regard the account she gave him of her time spent with Mrs Kubo as confidential, at least for the time being. Hanae was now off somewhere in Mrs Kubo's company, having telephoned ahead with some hesitation to suggest a further meeting. Mrs Kubo had accepted with alacrity, and had been waiting by the ticket barrier at the station when they arrived, as had the fair-haired, pipe-smoking Detective Sergeant Farrier. He had taken Otani and Noda first to Cambridge Police headquarters, but the conference there had been of little interest to Otani save for the further opportunity it gave him to spot similarities and differences as compared with the atmosphere of police premises in Japan.

The main problem for the police lay in the fact that Murakami's having been stabbed with a piece of cutlery belonging to St Cuthbert's College scarcely offset the overriding consideration that the Master's Lodge had been effectively open during the crucial time to any intruder. All the guests were in the garden, the front door was not only unlocked but wide open, and the few domestic staff who had been involved in handing round the simple refreshments were either collecting glasses or in the kitchen washing them.

In the days immediately following the murder they had all been closely questioned and none of them even remembered seeing Murakami pass through on the way to the cloakroom, much less any other person. On the face of it, there was no reason why an intruder could not have slipped in by the front door and lain in wait for Murakami. On the other hand, they were all agreed that Murakami's sudden rush to the lavatory had been on the spur of the moment and could scarcely have been predicted or planned.

"Unless someone put a powerful laxative in his drink," Noda had suggested facetiously to Farrier, without bothering to translate his remark for Otani's benefit.

Otani and Noda were convinced that the murderer had been present in the garden and had made an equally spontaneous decision to take advantage of an unexpected opportunity, following Murakami and seizing the first murder weapon which came to hand. On the handle of the knife the fingerprint officer had found such a miscellany of superimposed prints that the experts concluded that no useful information could be gained from them, beyond confirmation that the last person who had handled the knife had taken the precaution of picking it up while holding a paper napkin.

"We were talking about Dr Kubo and Dr Tawara," Otani prompted the Master cautiously when the old man paused to sip from his glass of sherry.

"Indeed, indeed. Just because the descendant of blacksmiths and your Mr Noda have gone off to interview others, we must not lose sight of the task in hand. Kubo and Tawara, yes. Good fellows, I'm sure . . . such a great pity they seem to have such a troubled relationship."

Otani thought he could see what the Master was driving at. "I haven't met either of them myself, but my wife spent some time in Tawara's company and that of a young girl, the daughter of the Kubos, I believe. I take it that Tawara is a married man?"

At this the Master's eyes opened wide and he chuckled. "You misunderstand me, Superintendent," he said, reaching for the decanter and re-filling both their glasses. Otani normally avoided wine of any kind, but was rapidly acquiring a taste for Cambridge sherry.

"I do not judge our friend Tawara to be a man likely to be much troubled by a sense of guilt over taking advantage of the infatuation of the Kubo child, or indeed that of any of the other ladies who have set their caps at him, including, I may say, the young lady's mother." He took out a white handkerchief and dabbed at his eyes with amusement. "I understand that Tawara has had a *most* successful stay in Cambridge from that point of view. In any case, there is no Mrs Tawara, neither here nor in Japan."

Otani waited quietly. He never believed in putting direct questions unless it became absolutely necessary.

"No, no. Of course it is quite possible that Kubo may fear that his daughter has fallen or will fall victim to Tawara's charms, but in that event he would hardly spend so much time in Tawara's company. It is, I fear, politics which divides them, and Tawara has the harder time of it. A sad business, a sad business. I recall that during the war we had the assistance of a similarly tormented man at Bletchley . . ." He must have noticed the bewilderment in Otani's expression, because he made a small gesture of irritation with himself.

"Forgive me, Superintendent. My discourtesy knows no bounds. Bletchley is the name of a place, not so very far from here as it happens, where a number of us were engaged during the war in the business of deciphering such military code traffic as we were able to intercept from those who were, sadly, our enemies. How few of us in Britain knew any Japanese in those days! Even those like myself who were more acquainted with the legends of the *Record of Ancient Things* and the names of the gods who created Japan than with the language of military formations and movements, even we were pressed into service."

Noda had told Otani on the train about the broad outlines

of Sir Benjamin Lincoln's wartime career as a code-breaker, so the Master's allusive remarks were much more comprehensible to him than would otherwise have been the case. "I see. I see. I was myself briefly involved with Naval Intelligence work," Otani said, and one bushy white eyebrow rose above the faded but still alert eyes.

"I would have supposed you too young a man," was all the Master said.

Otani shook his head quickly, and continued his oblique probing. "A *tormented* man. An interesting description." It had come as a surprise to Otani when Hanae had reported Mrs Kubo as having described Tawara as a Communst, and he had theorised to himself in any case after talking to Noda that the long arm of Japanese terrorist extremism would be more likely to reach out to kill Murakami through the agency of a Japanese than that of an English executioner. Now the Master too had spoken of politics in connection with Kubo and Tawara. With part of his mind Otani tried again to remember whether he had noticed any male Japanese who might have been either of them in the garden when Murakami passed through. Both Kubo's and Tawara's presence had been confirmed at the ceremony and the lunch afterwards.

Sir Benjamin raised his thin hands and dropped them again softly. "The word slipped out," he said. "I like Tawara very much. Kubo too, of course, but Tawara is the more interesting man. A good scientist, my colleagues tell me, and a personable fellow. Nevertheless, he reminds me of that other, the one I knew at Bletchley: not a Japanese, I may say, but a Chinese who knew your language. A handsome man, and a successful one with the ladies, too. Yet you know, one could almost as an ignorant bystander see the conflicting loyalties which tore at him and finally led to his breakdown. Poor fellow, poor fellow."

"A conflict of political loyalties, perhaps?"

"Political loyalties, political pressures, is there a difference? Let me try to make myself clearer,'' Sir Benjamin said helpfully. ''I like to practise my poor Japanese with scholars who come here from your country, and I have had many interesting conversations with both Kubo and Tawara. Men of their age would have been students in the mid-sixties, and I have from time to time quizzed them a little about the student uprisings in various parts of the world at that time. Including Japan, needless to say. I gained the impression that Tawara certainly, and Kubo very possibly, had been militants during the period of violence in Japan. Perhaps leaders.''

Otani smiled for thc first time since entering the Master's study that morning. ''So was my son-in-law. My daughter was one of his most fanatical supporters. I actually confronted him more than once. With tear-gas and water-cannon.''

''You amaze me, sir. You refer to Mr Shimizu who has played such a crucial role in the negotiations leading up to the establishment of our splendid Nantemo Institute of Japanese Studies?''

Otani nodded. ''Many of the ablest young men and women of their generation were well in the forefront of the rioting. Almost without exception they have become reconciled to the ways of our society; and those of us who were on the other side bear them no grudge.''

''Japanese society is indeed astonishingly tenacious towards its own,'' said the Master reflectively. ''Still I notice that you say '*almost* without exception'. There *are* exceptions, then?''

Otani found himself curiously reluctant to admit the fact and it was an effort to follow the lead which was opening up. ''A few,'' he acknowledged tersely. ''Some left Japan and became associated with terrorist organisations in other countries. Some are still there, active in radical politics. A few are in hiding, underground.''

''And what about those who in due course themselves

became university teachers? There must have been many in your country of mass higher education.'' It was the Master who was asking the questions, and Otani experienced a flicker of doubt as to whether decoding was the only thing he had done during the war.

Otani nodded slowly. ''Yes,'' he said at last. ''I understand what you mean. There have been cases where a university teacher has been put under pressure by groups with which he was formerly associated.'' He went on with even greater reluctance. ''One or two have been subjected to blackmail, or to physical violence. Even killed.''

''In recent years?''

''Yes.''

A light drizzle was falling outside, and the windows were closed. It was very quiet in the room as the swarthy Japanese in his humdrum suit and the old Englishman in tweeds looked at each other in a moment of perfect communication. Eventually it was Otani who broke the spell. ''I am deeply obliged to you,'' he said. ''I have committed an unpardonable intrusion into your precious time. You have been excessively courteous to me.'' He bowed from his seated position, then rose to his feet and the Master followed suit, graciously murmuring equally flowery phrases.

''You will join Madam now?'' Sir Benjamin asked in the entrance hall of the Master's Lodge as Otani emerged from the cloakroom in which Murakami had been killed by a ferocious and well-aimed thrust from a not-very-sharp dinner knife, having retrieved his umbrella from a stand in the corner not unlike the one in his own office in Kobe. The umbrella was one of his son-in-law's, of English make and lacking an automatic pop-up mechanism.

''Of course,'' the Master added as Otani confirmed that he was to join Hanae, ''I have no idea why anyone should wish harm to the late Mr Murakami . . . but no doubt you can think of a reason. My profound regards to Mrs Otani.''

Otani looked at him and wanted to smile, but had never

had any difficulty in his life in maintaining a poker face. "Thank you," he said. "I know the way."

After a final exchange of compliments and another bow as he turned at the outer gate and saw the old man with hand upraised at the great oaken front door, Otani marched off into the light rain. He *thought* he remembered the way to go, and it was agreeable to be walking all alone in Cambridge with plenty to think about.

Chapter 11

Kobe

INSPECTOR SAKAMOTO WAS A TRIAL TO ALL HIS SENIOR colleagues at Hyogo prefectural police Headquarters, not to mention his subordinates who uniformly detested the vinegary little martinet. He for his part was never quite sure which of his peers he regarded with the greater distaste, Kimura or Noguchi. As officer in charge of the Criminal Investigation Section he complained bitterly, frequently and almost always with complete justification to Otani about the way in which the other two trespassed into his domain, took it upon themselves to interfere in criminal cases, and even on numerous occasions availed themselves without prior consultation of the services of his staff.

On such occasions Otani would muster up a certain weary patience in hearing Sakamoto out and undertaking to look into the matter; but since he himself found the dried-up narrow-minded Inspector thoroughly unsympathetic he hardly convinced himself let alone Sakamoto. The idea of putting him in acting command of the Hyogo force during his absence had crossed Otani's mind only to be dismissed at once: it was ridiculous. Sakamoto was of course offended at having been passed over, but then he was generally offended about something, and it occurred to Otani at the time that it would do Kimura good to have to cope with him.

Mindful of Noguchi's furious reaction when he had impulsively tried to be overbearing, Kimura gave much anxious thought to the problem of how best he might detach Detective Woman Patrolman Junko Migishima from Sakamoto's section to undertake special duties. Her husband of almost a year was a member of Kimura's own staff, but in view of what Kimura had in mind, Migishima was the last person he could discuss the matter with. Nor could he face the idea of a straightforward discussion with Sakamoto. In the end therefore Kimura took the coward's way out and requested Sakamoto in a polite formal note to represent the Hyogo force at a National Police Agency conference in Tokyo on the problem of violent delinquency in junior high schools. Sakamoto accepted at once, the cold officialese of his reply not quite concealing his satisfaction, and was thus removed from the scene in Kobe for precisely the three days Kimura needed. Time enough to face the music when the thing was a *fait accompli*.

Junko Migishima herself was too tough a young woman to succumb to Kimura's charm alone, but listened carefully as he outlined his plan, her pert face alive with interest and with only an occasional flicker of doubt in her eyes. At twenty-four she looked good in her "office lady" clothes; like hundreds of thousands of other well-groomed, meticulously made-up girls of between eighteen and twenty-five who came tripping decorously out of offices and banks all over Japan at the end of each working day, some to attend classes in flower arrangement, others to practise the tea ceremony, and a great many to send off from time to time their written personal histories and statements of accomplishments and hobbies, with photographs, to relatives or well-placed family friends who would subsequently act as marriage brokers and arrange introductory meetings with young men looking for "cute, gentle" wives.

Her own marriage to Migishima had largely arranged itself, with Ninja Noguchi pressed into reluctant but proud service as a purely nominal go-between. Junko was undoubtedly cute, and her possession of a second *dan* qualification in the *aikido* art of unarmed combat did not necessarily deprive her of gentleness, but certainly she gave every indication of enjoying her work as a plain-clothes detective and none of wishing to retire to domestic life and motherhood.

There was a long silence after Kimura finished speaking, and Junko's questions, when they came, were methodical and practical. She had been jotting down notes in a small book she took from her handbag, and sat frowning at them as silence fell again. After a while Kimura could stand it no longer, and cleared his throat noisily. "Do you agree, then?" he asked eagerly when she looked up. "I would repeat that if you take this on, it will be as a volunteer. If you decline, we will forget the matter completely. I haven't discussed it with any other person, and . . . how shall I put this . . . I feel that it would be wiser if you did not mention it to your husband."

Junko grinned mischievously. "I'd have to think about that," she said, then put her notebook away and closed her bag with a decisive snap. "Very well, Inspector, I accept the assignment. Tomorrow at five, you say."

Kimura rose to his feet as she did, and bowed to her with respect. "Five," he confirmed. "You ought to go on board soon after four. Will you have time to prepare?"

Junko took a deep breath. Nervous tension showed for the first time, now that she had committed herself. "I think so," she said, and Kimura nodded encouragingly.

"I shall arrange for all possible back-up support for you. After all, a person like you who once acted as personal bodyguard for Prime Minister Mrs Thatcher in Tokyo can carry off a job like this, I'm quite sure."

Kimura had even gone to the un-Japanese extreme of opening the door for her as he finished speaking, and Junko left the room just as Noguchi was about to enter it from the corridor. He said nothing until she had gone and he had entered. "What was that about Thatcher?" he then enquired.

"Don't you remember, Ninja? Migishima-san was one of the team of women police they put together specially to guard Mrs Thatcher during the summit conference in Tokyo."

"What, when she went to the toilet?" Kimura ignored Noguchi's crudity and led the way to the easy-chairs so recently occupied by Junko Migishima and himself.

"Now, I don't expect you to approve of what I've done," he began disarmingly, "but I've been thinking of this Inland Sea cruise business."

"You're not going," Noguchi said promptly. "It was bad enough taking the chances you did at Yamamoto's funeral ceremonies."

"I'm not planning to go, Ninja. Just hear me out, please. It's unique chance for us. *Yakuza* bosses have staged these things before. Chartering a ferry for an overnight cruise among the islands in the Inland Sea. It was you who told me about it a couple of times. The daimyo himself, with forty or fifty bosses of affiliated groups and senior back-up men and twice that number of strippers and bar hostesses for the fun and games. But this one is different. The daimyo's cabin will be empty. This cruise is going to provide the setting for an extended meeting of the eight members of the presidium and the decisive discussions between Shiraishi and Uchibori for the succession."

Noguchi rasped a right hand over his stubbly chin. "So? There's always confidential talk among bosses on those jaunts. That's why they go on a boat. Not just because they don't want the vice squad spoiling their party."

"Of course. It's a very secure arrangement," Kimura agreed. "All the same, this *is* different. You and I don't believe either Shiraishi or Uchibori will agree on a carve-up of the Yamamoto empire. One or other's going to decide to go for the big one and carry the majority of the presidium with him. We need to get someone in on those talks."

Noguchi was still unforthcoming, but shifted slightly in his chair. "Thought about it," he admitted. "Already contacted one of the crew. Not much use, though. Barman, he is. Thought they might get a bit careless with a few whiskies inside. Might do, I suppose. Shiraishi and Uchibori certainly won't be talking big stuff in the bar, though, and my barman won't be going to their cabins."

"Ah, that's an excellent move, though," Kimura said with excessive enthusiasm, still trying to soften Noguchi up before coming clean with him. "There's no knowing what some of the small fry might come out with." He beamed with more than a trace of nervousness. "Actually, it had occurred to me that there would almost certainly be a mah-jong gambling session at some stage, very possibly in one of the top bosses' cabins, and if so they'll want to do it right, with a woman or two to help run it."

Noguchi's expression was neutral, but his whole posture suggested wariness as Kimura took a deep breath and went on. "Well, I've just been talking as you see to Migishima-san—"

At the sound of the name Noguchi sat bolt upright and his eyes flicked fully open. "No," he said flatly. "That kid's not available." He sat there glaring at Kimura, who looked at him first in embarrassment, then in mute appeal, and finally with solemn gravity as he realised that probably nothing he could say would reconcile Noguchi to the idea that the young woman in relation to whom he now stood as a kind of godfather should in effect be handed over to the sordid clutches of a crowd of drunken hoodlums.

When Kimura did speak at last, it was quietly and with a certain assurance, and Noguchi listened. "I was quite aware that you would disapprove of this idea, Ninja, and that was why I took the precaution of discussing it with Migishima-san first. I want to make it clear that there was at no time any question of simply assigning her to this job. As you know perfectly well, our women colleagues on the criminal investigation side are frequently required to act as decoys. Sometimes we're in a position to call for volunteers, but quite often they simply have to do as they're told. And they do so, as part of the job." Kimura paused and delicately sipped some of the tepid green tea left in his cup from earlier.

"However, I gave this young officer every possible opportunity to back out, but she freely volunteered to help us. As it happens, she is probably the most resourceful and physically the toughest girl in the Hyogo force and she certainly won't come to any harm. In the role of a gambling madam she might have to watch some sex, but she won't be expected to take part. I'm sorry Ninja, but the plan will go forward. I've already authorised it. The fact that you're close to the Migishimas doesn't give either of them special privileges as police officers."

Noguchi twitched and seemed about to speak, then flung a look of pure hatred at Kimura as he hauled himself up out of his chair and went over to the door, slamming it behind him as he left the room without a backward glance.

Kimura sat back and closed his eyes in weariness. Although convinced of the viability of his scheme, he was not particularly happy about involving Junko Migishima in it. He believed what he had told Noguchi, though. There would be no particular problem for Junko getting on board the ship. Kimura was confident that she would dress appropriately, and girls would be converging from bars, strip shows and Turkish bath-houses all over Kobe. All except Junko would be known to some at least of the others, and possibly to one or two of the gangsters on board, but it would call for little ingenuity on her part to melt into the crowd.

It would be trickier for Junko to establish her credentials as a gambler, since women of that type constitute something of an élite: that was up to her, and Kimura knew of no woman officer more likely to succeed. What was certain was that if either Shiraishi or Uchibori took a fancy to her, she would have the chance to be alone with one of the two serious claimants to the throne vacated by the death of Yamamoto and some faint possibility of being able to establish the link with the murdered philanthropist Murakami.

Kimura was certain of one thing, which was that if Otani had been in charge the situation by now would look completely different. He wished he could make up his mind whether or not he was glad that Otani was so far away from the action.

Chapter 12

Cambridge—London

THE RAIN HAD DIED AWAY, AND THE AIR SMELT DAMP but fresh and clean as Otani stood with Hanae on the platform at Cambridge Station waiting for the fast train to Liverpool Street. He was uneasy about their travelling alone, but Hanae seemed entirely confident of her ability to manage not only the necessary negotiations with the railway staff, but also to get them by Underground to St John's Wood without the aid of Noda, who had decided to remain in Cambridge for further talks with Sergeant Farrier and his colleagues.

"It's late," Otani said for the third time. "Are you sure we're on the right platform?" Hanae pointed to the indicator board and Otani peered at it obediently, missing the torrent of information which issues almost continuously from loudspeakers on every Japanese railway station.

"Trains are sometimes late in Japan, too," she reasoned.

"Not very often," Otani grumbled in reply. "Which way will it come? Why don't they put the names of the next stations on either side, like we do?" They had come to a kind of unspoken agreement to avoid talking about their experiences in Cambridge until safely on board the train, which now at last came into view.

Otani again experienced a pang of nostalgia for the orderliness of Japanese railways when he realised that the platform on which they stood lacked white lines and numbers to indicate precisely where the doors would open to admit passengers. Nor was there the strip of special surfacing with low studs to provide a kind of braille guide for the blind to read with their feet, and no amplified voice warned them to stand back as the train pulled in. Otani commented on all this to Hanae, who merely observed rather tartly that it was no doubt because English people were less addicted than Japanese to committing suicide by throwing themselves in front of trains and did not need to be treated like children by being told what to do every minute of the day.

Having decided that he himself was in any case thoroughly ambivalent about his reactions to English ways, Otani merely raised an eyebrow and forebore to draw attention to the inconvenience of having to open the compartment door for oneself. He had already caused amusement by bumping his nose quite painfully against a glass door at the hotel which disobligingly failed to open itself at his approach as a self-respecting Japanese glass door would.

There was however no doubt that the interior of the train was more comfortable than those they were used to, and he and Hanae settled themselves down in their first-class seats with sighs of contentment. Otani decided to stop worrying and to assume that they were on the right train, even though nobody seemed anxious to tell them so, and turned to Hanae with a brief smile as the train gathered speed.

"Well then," he said. "You had an interesting morning." It was a statement rather than a question, but Hanae nodded anyway, eyes wide and amused. "So did I," Otani went on, quite unconsciously drifting into an approach he often employed, that of embarking on a narrative of his own with only an occasional question to draw out from another person information he sought.

"As long as Noda and I were with the Master and the local police officer it was rather tedious, but afterwards we did quite well. I had a good talk with Sir Lincoln." He had not understood Noda's explanation of the correct form of address for the head of St Cuthbert's, and had throughout his encounter with the Master addressed him as "Saa Rinkon", which appeared to occasion Sir Benjamin no surprise.

"Then we double-checked the guest list for the reception and the names of everybody in the procession, and I must say it all seems to me to suggest that Tawara or Kubo . . . did you see the daughter? What was her name, Kumiko?"

"Tomoko." Hanae was smiling. "No, she wasn't there. We talked about her again quite a lot, though. Her mother's still worried about her, is she?" Hanae's smile faded and she looked at him thoughtfully. "You don't really think the Kubos are mixed up in this business, do you?"

Otani was looking out of the compartment towards the corridor, a speculative expression on his face. "I'm surprised the girl hasn't come round with a trolley by now," he muttered inconsequentially. "I'd like a coffee or something."

"There was no trolley on the train this morning," Hanae said firmly. "There might be a buffet car, perhaps." Otani sank back, disappointed. Besides coffee an errant vision of one of those little pork pies had in spite of his comparatively recent lunch strayed across his consciousness.

"It's amazing how unobservant people are," he said after a while, ignoring Hanae's earlier question about the Kubos. "Of course, the police have had to move carefully in asking the English people present if they noticed anyone leave the garden. They didn't want to show their hand too obviously. Most of them couldn't remember, and do you know, two of them said the same thing, that Japanese all look alike."

"How extraordinary!" Hanae was genuinely surprised, and mentally contrasted the beloved, often stern face of her husband to the lean, much paler features of Tawara under his shock of prematurely grey hair, turned as they had been to Tomoko who was looking up at him hungrily as they walked away after the outing in the punt.

Otani went on reflectively. "Noda could be more open with the Japanese businessmen when he saw them in London yesterday. Would you believe that four different people were named as having left the garden as the procession was forming up—apart from Noda and me, of course?"

"What about Dr Tawara and Dr Kubo? Were they in the four?"

Otani nodded. "Yes. I wanted to interview both of them today, but Tawara was at the Low Temperature Institute involved in some complicated experiment, I was told, and Kubo's gone to London."

"Yes. Mrs Kubo told me. She said he goes twice a month, to do research at the British Museum Library."

"Anyway Noda's trying to fix a time for me to see both of them." Otani looked out of the window at the empty Essex fields, to him almost unimaginably huge after the tiny holdings of farmers in Japan. "The Cambridge police made a chance to talk to Tomoko though. Made it seem casual, didn't tell her parents." He sucked his teeth. "Very irregular. Well, she was very insistent that Tawara never left the garden, and was in fact talking to her while the procession was being organised. Very insistent. Too insistent.

"Alibis can be broken. Three other people think Tawara might have left the garden—and two think Kubo did. I wish I could remember myself, but I can't. And you said you can't." Hanae nodded. "A child like Tomoko won't be able to sustain a simple lie for very long if that's what it is. Tawara's strongest point so far is the absence of motive. Why would a respected scientist suddenly take it into his head to kill a man—on the spur of the moment—that he's never set eyes on before? True he's from our part of Japan, as Murakami was, but you can't attach any importance to that. There must be ten million people living in the Kansai area around Kobe, Kyoto and Osaka. Then we've got Mrs Kubo's remark about Tawara s politics. It doesn't amount to much."

"All the same, you think the evidence points more to Dr Tawara." Hanae spoke in a matter-of-fact way. She had heard her husband reason in this apparently perverse manner before.

"Well, it might," Otani conceded. "It was the Master who convinced me that we really need more information about his background and possible connections. Noda's going to check through the Japanese Embassy channels to Tokyo." He compressed his lips and sighed heavily. "It's a pity. I wish I could be in two places at once. I could handle this perfectly well with Kimura and Noguchi to help."

Hanae patted his hand. "We're on holiday, remember?" Otani pulled a face at her but his heart wasn't in it, and he soon relapsed into brooding silence which persisted until the train pulled in under the great Victorian fretted roof of Liverpool Street Station, eight minutes late.

Then Otani was again all timidity and hesitation as Hanae led the way with a confidence more apparent than real towards the Underground, announcing that they were to change to the Jubilee Line at Bond Street. Although Hanae's spoken English was almost non-existent, she read the Roman alphabet with reasonable ease, smiling as Otani pored over each word with painful concentration, mouthing each uncouth sound to himself. Although maintaining the most uncompromising air of disbelief and mistrust, Otani watched while Hanae battled with the huge cumbersome ticket machine, then suffered himself to be led to the platform Hanae indicated and to board the train which shortly stopped there. It was the rush hour; not so spectacular as in Tokyo or Osaka, though the Otanis had little enough experience of either, but there were enough standing passengers for them to be pushed near the doorway, where Otani insisted on remaining in case they should miss their stop.

The change at Bond Street was negotiated without too much trouble, and Hanae pointed in triumph at the station name "St John's Wood" in the list on the platform indicator, after they had both looked in vain for a telephone by means of which to warn Akiko that they would soon be home. St John's Wood looked positively homely and welcoming in the early evening as they made their way from the station, and when they arrived at the flat Otani airily shrugged off Akiko's compliments to him on the skill with which he had navigated the pair of them on their perilous journey from Cambridge.

There was a message for him from Noda, who had telephoned from Cambridge about an hour earlier to ask Otani to meet him for dinner at eight at a restaurant in Hampstead, where it seemed he lived. Akiko had already accepted on his behalf, and to Otani's great relief had already booked a minicab to take him there. Hanae was diverted by the lofty man-about-town manner he assumed as he changed his clothes and prepared to go out again so soon after returning from Cambridge, and judged that whatever frustrations he might be experiencing over having to assume a peripheral role in the Murakami murder investigation, he was thoroughly relishing being in demand and hobnobbing not only with the Master of St Cuthbert's but also with a Japanese diplomat who she had already privately decided had responsibilities beyond those he claimed for himself in public.

She and Akiko passed a pleasant evening after Otani had left for his engagement with Noda. There was of course Kazuo to fuss over, and an exhaustive discussion of his future education should the Shimizus remain on the international circuit. There was a simple meal including Japanese specialities which, Akiko explained to Hanae's surprise, could be bought quite conveniently nearby at one of several Japanese food stores, and then a television play which quite intrigued Hanae by reason of its sexual explicitness. It was quite different from "Adults Hour" shown on Saturday nights in Japan, she and Akiko agreed.

No reference was made to the absence of Akiko's husband. Even though Hanae knew that he was unlike the majority of young businessmen in that when in Japan he rarely went out drinking with his colleagues, preferring to keep his private life private, she simply assumed that his new work in London would involve him in evening engagements most days. In fact, Akiko had simply omitted to mention that her husband was to join Noda and her father at the restaurant.

It was after eleven, and the two women were talking vaguely about going to bed when in the quiet of the late evening they heard the lift stop outside the flat and raucous laughter followed by an ineffectual scraping at the door. Akiko crossed and opened it, to reveal Shimizu making passes at the air with his key while Otani hummed a little tune to himself, a foolish smile on his face, which was flushed brick red, and displaying a large smudge of lipstick on his shirt collar.

They were not in fact helplessly drunk: merely in that state when everything either of them said struck the other as being brilliantly witty, and Hanae knew quite well that there was no point in reproaching them that night. Akiko was less philosophical and, though she ignored her father, treated Shimizu to a blistering account of his shortcomings to which he listened owlishly, before beginning to conduct her like an orchestra, which made matters worse.

By the time Hanae got Otani to bed, he was reasonably tractable and quiet, and she fully expected him to sleep solidly before waking up with a hangover the next morning. It came as a great surprise when at about three her own light sleep was interrupted by his sliding carefully out of bed. He left the door open and she heard him in the living room, dialling a very long series of numbers on the telephone. She realised that it would be about eleven in the morning in Japan.

Chapter 13

The Inland Sea

THE WELL-APPOINTED CRUISE VESSEL WAS CALLED THE *Tosa Maru* and boarding her that afternoon constituted no problem at all for Junko. Special charter arrangements for Inland Sea cruises were not unusual. At the time indeed they were enjoying a certain vogue in the case of some of the bigger employers in Osaka and Kobe as providing a novel variation on the traditional annual company outing; a change from bus tours to beauty spots or the temporary take-over of a hotspring resort hotel. For the officers and regular crew members such scenic cruises made a pleasant change from routine scheduled sailings to ports in Shikoku and Kyushu.

The larger ferries were in any case little more than floating hotel/restaurants, and with the connivance of the crew, numbers of girls made their way on board whenever their contacts in the shipping line offices let them know that there would be a great preponderance of men among the passengers. They did profitable business even on ostensibly respectable cruises, and when word went round that this charter had been arranged by an affiliate of the Yamamoto organisation there was no need for a special recruitment effort to ensure an adequate turnout of bar hostesses, Turkish bath masseuses and strippers.

Junko turned up at the pier smartly dressed in Western clothes, a severely styled wig transforming her normally tousled, cheerfully healthy appearance, carrying a small case in which was her other gear. It was a simple matter to attach herself to a band of three obvious bar hostesses, who climbed giggling up the gangway to the passenger entry where a steward gave them a knowing wink and waved them to a big cabin in the first-class section. This was done up in Japanese style with *tatami* matting as flooring, and normally functioned as a banqueting room, but had evidently been set aside as a changing room for the occasion. A few girls were already kneeling in front of low dressing-tables seeing to their makeup.

Within minutes more new arrivals appeared on the scene, and such was her strength of character that they all seemed to take it for granted that Junko was there in some kind of supervisory role. One or two actually remarked to her as they sorted out their belongings that it was their first experience of a cruise assignment, and asked Junko to advise them as necessary. No incongruity was apparent to a soul in the room as Junko gravely and courteously bowed to one young girl who was half into her sole garment, a gaudy sequinned minidress, and they each requested the other's favour in the conventional phrases, even though at the same time other girls were exchanging bawdy wisecracks of the most explicit kind.

There was plenty of room in the cabin for the thirty or so women who eventually assembled there, and Junko's dominance was assured when she slipped out of her own clothes to change into the scarlet silk underskirt and light but boldly decorated kimono she had brought with her.

The police artist had done a brilliant job on her right arm, shoulder and back. A multi-coloured Chinese dragon wound its way over Junko's slender body, its long red snake-like tongue licking with lascivious delicacy down just barely to flick at her nipple. It had been a long job, and for Junko an embarrassing morning in spite of the artist's unconcerned and professionally polite manner as she sat there nude to the waist in his small, untidy office. To take her mind off the curious but finally not disagreeable ordeal, she had spent much of the time watching police video tapes of illegal high-stakes mah-jong sessions, noting the facial expressions of the haughty madams who presided, and memorising some of the phrases they used. When it was at last finished, Junko had great confidence in the painted false tattoo. She was sure that it would pass all but the closest scrutiny, which she had no intention of permitting.

"Waah! *Kakui!* Fantastic!" The compliments of the girls nearest to Junko were quite sincere, and she slipped even more securely into her assumed role when one of them asked quite innocently which mah-jong club she ran. Some of the other women had small tattoos on their thighs or shoulders but to Junko's relief she saw none who bore the same tiny lozenge device as the artist had painted on her own thigh to mark her as one of Yamamoto's women.

Junko had herself chosen that particular mark from the book of specimen photographs kept in Criminal Investigation Section at headquarters after careful thought, and hoped that she had done the right thing. The dragon at least was correct: only the more successful gambling madams bore them on their bodies for display at the right moment when the stakes were high enough.

The miniature tape-recorder was already sewn into her *obi* sash and could be switched on at any time Junko chose to fiddle with the fastening in a gesture all women in Japanese dress perform consciously or unconsciously a dozen times a day; and although she fully expected to remain tense and scared throughout her hours on the ferry, Junko took certain satisfaction in what she had achieved in the first hour when she made her way out of the cabin and took a look round the ship which was then under way.

It was a large vessel, built to accommodate a hundred or so first-class and three or four times that number of second-class passengers on voyages which would usually last several hours and from time to time take a full two days, when the route was to Okinawa in the far south. The dining-rooms, bars and public lounges were beginning to fill up with flashily-suited men, some already red-faced with drink, and many with lighted cigarettes held in the teeth, lips drawn back in a caricature of professional menace. Most were young, in their twenties, though here and there was an older man, usually accompanied by two or more sycophantic juniors.

The bars were busy, though service was fast because all drinks were free, unlike the electronic games which nevertheless attracted a good many addicts, including some of the girls. Junko had no trouble while on her tour of observation in fending off the few men who approached her. In spite of her youth, she successfully employed the combination of ribaldry and brisk good-humour typical of the bar mamma-sans she had observed in action in the course of previous plain-clothes assignments; and she maintained the impression of being in authority over the other girls by adjudicating a minor dispute when two men began to quarrel over the same girl, who herself appeared to be quite indifferent as to which of the two of them should take her to see the pornographic film show which had just been announced as starting in ten minutes in the TV lounge. Junko was able to summon a second girl without difficulty, and the four trooped off together in tipsy good fellowship.

Junko herself then went on deck. The ship was cruising on a southerly course a mile or two off the east coast of Awaji island, and it was dusk. The last stains of sunset were still in the sky, and the low wooded hills had taken on the quality of a Chinese ink painting, layers of soft purple-grey rising one above the other as lights began to wink out from the shoreline. Junko paused to take in the tranquility, and noticed a girl leaning on the rail not far away from her, gazing at the sea. She was young; probably no more than eighteen, and the painted face looked troubled and vulnerable as the breeze ruffled her hair. Junko could see and in her imagination hear the child sigh as she turned away at last and made her way back to the sordid vulgarity below decks.

There were very few people about. The officers on the bridge had obviously decided to quarantine themselves for the duration of the cruise, and the stewards were too busy plying the gangsters with drink to have time to themselves. Junko had not expected to see either of her two possible targets at close quarters until later, and it was something of a bonus when a group of men emerged through one of the heavy wooden doors and she recognised Shiraishi and Uchibori among them from the photographs of presidium members she had studied intently in the set shown to her by Kimura.

It would not in any case have been difficult to deduce that these were the two senior barons on board from the number and superior style of their escorts, but Junko's task of identification was made easier by the fact that the two bosses turned and appeared to exchange a few words with the members of their respective retinues, after which they moved off together, the bodyguards following at a distance of five metres or so.

The promenade deck was well lit, and as Uchibori and Shiraishi passed close to Junko she saw them both clearly, and without a moment's hesitation decided that Ubichori was the man to mark. She heard nothing of their conversation since both fell silent as soon as they spotted her, but Junko could see the sweat on Shiraishi's face and the contained strength in Uchibori's. She noted too the cool, relaxed way in which he gave her a long, appraising look as they passed. Not for the first time that day Junko was glad that her chosen role entailed that she should maintain a certain air of superior disdain, and she met his eyes boldly.

Uchibori was probably in his forties; ten years or so younger than Shiraishi and surprisingly youthful to have achieved so much power already, since in gangster circles rules of seniority are observed which are not greatly different from those which prevail in more orthodox walks of life. He was a big, loosely built man, with greying hair styled in a crewcut. His features were strongly modelled, and the thought flashed through Junko's mind that he looked a little like the American movie star Paul Newman.

The pause was very brief and soon the two moved on. Junko ducked out of the way of their following escort, just too late to avoid being waylaid by one of them who demanded to know her name. There was no point in creating an unnecessary potential hazard for herself, so she gave her real name, Junko, though not her family name. It could cause nothing but complications if in a moment of stress she failed to answer to an invented one.

"Are you from the White Cross Club?"

This time Junko was even more wary. "Could be," she said and the man scratched his nose, wondering.

"I heard they've got someone special there," he said at last. "Look, don't set up any games for a while. My boss might be interested." Junko was pleased at being taken so readily for a gambling madam, but couldn't understand why, until the man reached out and delicately adjusted a fold of her kimono at the neck. He even went so far as to smile crookedly at her. "Keep it covered up—for now," he said. "The tattoo. Where can I find you later?" His eyes were focused beyond her, and Junko guessed that the two bosses were coming back.

"I'll be around," she said casually as she skipped to one side and looked for a convenient door.

Junko needed to think, and took refuge in a nearby ladies' room. First she checked that part of the false tattoo was indeed just visible at her neckline and began to tighten her kimono to conceal it, but then thought again and let it be. The sight of it by others had brought her nothing but advantage thus far, after all.

The police dossiers on Shiraishi and Uchibori had indicated that both men had extensive interests in gambling syndicates, but said nothing about their personal tastes. The hugely popular game of mah-jong constituted far and away the biggest potential area for illegal gaming. The legitimate clubs where office workers and students went at lunchtime and the early evening made good enough profits for their operators even in the ordinary way of business, and routinely came under *yakuza* protection arrangements; but the big money came from a handful of very discreetly run establishments based in private houses and flats, where in surroundings of opulent luxury "special members" could play for high stakes.

They came from an unlikely medley of occupations. Some, like the real-estate developers and the politicians were well enough aware of the fact that a substantial rake-off from all the stakes went to the house. Other patrons were themselves gangsters from affiliated organisations who tended to regard it as a sort of privilege to lose money on the premises: sometimes indeed they won. The doctors and wealthy businessmen who made up the numbers, with now and again a TV actor or pop star drifting briefly into orbit, pretended to ignore the illegality of what they were doing, or sometimes elaborated eloquent arguments about the ridiculous oppressiveness of the law. They were safe enough, and they knew it.

In the unlikely event of a police raid, it would be the known *yakuza* who would be most vulnerable. With the Penal Code of Japan specifying a three-year term of imprisonment for gambling or betting as a habitual practice and five years for assembling gamblers and maintaining premises for the purpose, the police had a convenient catch-all to use when they wanted to pick up a particular man. The well-heeled or glamorous punters from the straight world had all the assurances they needed that witnesses would be forthcoming who would if necessary swear that they were present as innocent guests or spectators. Junko knew that from personal experience, having done under-cover observation jobs from time to time in the guise of an aspiring TV actress.

Junko's chances of success in gaining access to either Shiraishi or Uchibori, and preferably to the latter, depended to a considerable extent on their having a personal taste for high-stake play; and it was not until late that evening that she discovered that they did.

By that time Junko had mingled with a number of groups of men and had picked up useful information merely by keeping her ears open. For the small fry among the *yakuza* on board the cruise was purely and simply a spree, with booze and girls on hand for their benefit. Predictably, a number of them had passed out on sofas or staggered off to the cabins with temporary companions, and as the evening wore on the numbers thinned.

This made it all the easier for Junko to circulate through the lounges and home in on some of the petty bosses who were inclined to hold court at tables, and whose bragging and indiscreet talk gave Junko several nuggets of information as she solicitously poured their whisky and lit their cigarettes for them and deftly diverted their wandering hands towards the girls who were being paid to cope with them.

Once or twice Junko thought it worth switching on the tape recorder, and by the time the summons did come she was desperately tired but had ample confirmation that the smart money was on Uchibori to inherit the overall control of the Yamamoto network, as well as several references to the timely removal of a third shadowy contender from outside the presidium who could only be Yamamoto's former secret associate Murakami.

Junko was not sure how long he had been there staring at her. She was at a table littered with overflowing ashtrays and dirty glasses, listening with a bored weariness she had no need to affect to a vulgarian with a mouthful of gold teeth holding forth to three attentive acolytes and two sleepy bar-girls about his lucrative hold over various municipal contracts in the administrative capital of a nearby prefecture. During the evening a noisy background hubbub had developed to which her ear had become attuned, and it was the comparative silence which fell on the whole room which made Junko turn her head. The raucous disco-style taped music played on, but all conversation died away.

Then she saw him, several metres away but unmistakably staring at her. Uchibori had changed into a blue and white cotton yukata, and wore straw sandals on his otherwise bare feet. The narrow sash was tied low on his hips, and he looked powerful and confident. The provincial boss next to her nudged Junko uneasily. "Go on," he muttered. "You're wanted." There was not much doubt about it, and Junko snapped into full alertness as the adrenalin surged into her blood-stream. Uchibori scarcely moved his head as his eyes flickered, but the almost imperceptible gesture was as compelling as a physical blow, and Junko stood up and went over to him.

He turned and led the way out of the lounge, with Junko following, and said nothing until they were in the passageway leading to the "special de luxe" cabins normally booked by honeymoon couples. "Wasting your time," Uchibori said then. "That trash play for cigarette money." He opened a door to disclose another *tatami* matted cabin in which a mah-jong game was in progress. There were three men in the cabin, Shiraishi among them. The mark of failure was upon him, even though he sprawled like a gross potentate groping at the drunken girls who were pawing him and the other men.

There was money all over the floor, and as Junko took in the scene one of the other men picked up several ten-thousand yen notes from the untidy pile at his side and thrust them down the front of a giggling girl's kimono. Uchibori growled a few words and a semblance of order was restored with Junko installed as directress of the gambling. She knew the curt jargon of the game and snapped out her arrogant instructions with casual authority, conscious of Uchibori's eyes upon her.

She was sure that they were the only two people in the cabin who were not stupid with drink, even though Uchibori drank several glasses of the finest Suntory Royal whisky during the next hour, while Shiraishi produced more and more money from the sleeves of his yukata and grunted and sweated with fuddled concentration. The stakes were indeed high, and Uchibori and one other man who was clearly his own associate were winning most of the time. They were generous to Junko who accumulated by way of tips an amount she later discovered to be equivalent to more than six months' worth of police pay.

It began to look as though Shiraishi had almost had enough, and with an inward gulp of apprehension Junko made her own most dangerous move. Slipping her hand through the opening under her kimono sleeve she wrenched the upper part of the garment completely off her right shoulder as she had seen it done by gambling madams at the moment of truth, when they judged it right to enter the game themselves. The lurid tattoo was fully exposed, and there was an audible intake of breath even on the part of Uchibori.

Shiraishi goggled and produced what must have been his last stack of banknotes, and the other men made themselves ready. The clatter of the tiles had a brittle, feverish quality and it was all over in a few minutes. Shiraishi was pale and looked ill as he watched his money go, but it was Uchibori's own man who precipitated a crisis, when with a whoop of triumph he pushed one of the complaisant girls onto her back and fumblingly tried to mount her.

Then Uchibori moved with the speed of a snake striking, seizing the man by the hair and yanking his head back so violently that Junko heard a distinct crack. It sobered him up remarkably, and he shuffled out of the cabin without looking back. The mah-jong session was clearly over, and after a brief silence Shiraishi and his man gathered up what little money they still possessed, their cigarettes and lighters, and made off also.

The girls were still there, looking bewildered except for the one on her back who had gone to sleep with her legs still splayed. Junko shook her awake as she covered the girl's body and told her companions to take her away, calling one of them back to straighten the litter of bottles, glasses and ashtrays. Then Junko was alone with Uchibori and she was frightened.

She had earlier allowed her kimono to part to afford him a glimpse of the Yamamoto lozenge mark on her thigh, and was not therefore surprised by his first question, put in a quiet conversational manner as she slipped her arm back into the sleeve and adjusted the kimono round her body. Uchibori had made no attempt to take advantage of her semi-nudity, but Junko had felt almost physically burned when his eyes had been on her exposed breast.

"Who's paying you now that Yamamoto's dead?"

"He took care of me," she said, keeping her voice clipped and hard. "Besides, I can make a living." She nodded at the pile of banknotes beside her, and Uchibori casually picked up a stack of his own and tossed them on the pile, nodding approval as Junko stowed the whole lot away in her sleeve. Then he reached for the bottle nearest him and splashed whisky into his own and another glass before he spoke again.

"Have a drink." It was a command rather an invitation, and Junko reached for the glass and took the smallest possible sip from it as he watched her.

"You won," she said flatly.

"The game? Of course."

"No, everything. You're the new daimyo."

She had switched on the tape-recorder when tidying her kimono. It would give her perhaps forty-five minutes' recording time. "I intend to be." Uchibori's manner was still controlled.

"Do you expect Shiraishi to put up a fight?" Junko tried to keep her voice steady, and was rewarded with a blank stare from Uchibori. Then he laughed, drained his glass, opened the lower part of his yukata and beckoned, pointing at himself rather crudely.

Junko felt the colour rising in her cheeks as she saw his erection, but even managed a wink. "Later," she murmured.

It was a dangerous moment, and Junko was glad when he relaxed slightly and sprawled back on the *zabuton* cushions behind him. "Shiraishi's a loser," he said. "He never had a real chance. Just pushing his luck."

It was now or never. "What about Yamamoto's partner?"

Uchibori sat up slowly and looked at Junko with something like respect in his expression. "Yamamoto told you about him? Surely you never saw them together?"

"Who, Yamamoto and Murakami? No, of course not." It seemed to Junko that she blurted the name in a false, strident way, but Uchibori rose to the bait.

"Murakami might have been a problem," he said, "but he went on a trip overseas. You might say I cancelled his return ticket—just a long-distance call was all it needed." Again Junko saw the dominant male sexuality in his eyes, and this time allowed herself to be pulled towards him and kissed, but drew back when he seized her hand and dragged it towards his penis.

"Impatient," she murmured, sliding the hand up instead to his head and tugging playfully at his hair. "Let a girl get ready, won't you? There's a ladies' room just across the passage. Two minutes. It'll be worth it to you . . . why don't you put some bedding down while I'm gone?" The husky sexuality of her voice was far from contrived, and Junko's heart was thudding and lurching. Uchibori was a disturbingly attractive man.

Much more so than the captain of the ship who finally, after Junko succeeded in arriving at the bridge unobserved, agreed after an incredulous inspection of her warrant card and a radio telephone call to the Acting Commander of the Hyogo Prefectural Police, to give her refuge for the remainder of the night in the officers' quarters, and locked the tape-recorder away in the safe in his own cabin.

Chapter 14

London

OTANI LEANED BACK IN THE LEATHER CHAIR AND thoughtfully flipped through Dr Kubo's passport. "Good of you to come in, Dr Kubo," he said. "I hope it wasn't inconvenient." Otani still had something of a headache at two-thirty in the afternoon following his night out, but had been able to forget about it during most of the day, occupied as it had been in planning this moment. It probably made his expression even grimmer than it usually was in repose, but this was no bad thing.

Dr Kubo's glasses flashed as he looked round the room, and he clutched at his leather document case as though it were a life-belt. "All the way from Cambridge," Otani added. He had left the passports of Mrs Kubo and Tomoko on the desk between them.

"The message from the Embassy said it was urgent. A special endorsement needed. My wife was quite alarmed when she received the message, and you weren't particularly informative when I telephoned back to check with you." Dr Kubo's Adam's apple bobbed up and down in his thin neck as he spoke.

"It's more of a check, really, Dr Kubo," Otani said, "on all Japanese citizens who were present at the opening ceremony for the Nantemo Institute of Japanese Studies at Cambridge recently. We just wanted to make sure that the papers of everyone concerned are perfectly in order. Yours especially." Otani let the words hang in the air between them.

Kubo assumed an entirely credible expression of bewildered irritation, mingled with an element of added wariness. "Why ours especially?"

'Tell me about Dr Tawara, would you? Otani asked, ignoring Kubo's question and leaning forward in a businesslike way, like a bank manager discussing a loan application. "Did you first meet him in Cambridge, or back in Japan?"

Kubo blinked behind his glasses. "What business is that of the Consul's?" Kubo took off his glasses and polished them with jerky mechanical movements of his hands.

"Ah, that's the point," Otani said gently. "This is the Consul's office, but I'm not the Consul. I'm a police officer, as a matter of fact. I must apologise for getting you here under a pretext, but you were away from Cambridge yesterday, and in any case it's better Tawara shouldn't know I wanted to ask you a few questions about him. In connection with the death of Shigeru Murakami."

As with all people who habitually wear glasses, Kubo's eyes looked vague and blank without his, and Otani was unable to read what he was thinking. When he did put them back on, there was only neutral caution in Kubo's face. "What makes you think Tawara might have anything to do with that?"

Otani shrugged. "Routine enquiries, Dr Kubo. I'm handling the interviews with Japanese, but the English people are seeing many others who were at St Cuthbert's College that day."

Otani let the pause go on as long as Kubo wanted, and

was not surprised by the question that came. ''Have you interviewed Tawara yet?''

Otani shook his head. ''Not yet. Tell me about him. Do you think he'd be likely to know a man like Murakami?''

Kubo cleared his throat fussily. ''Of course, I wish to cooperate with the authorities in any way I can,'' he began. Otani found himself disliking the man's precise, academic manner of speech. ''I find it distasteful to be required to speak about a colleague in this way, however. Dr Tawara is a scientist of some standing, while I am a specialist in English literature.''

''Thomas Hardy,'' said Otani, nodding, and succeeding in giving the completely false impression that he was familiar with the name.

''Precisely. Our academic paths therefore never cross, but I see a certain amount of him, as a member of our small Japanese community in Cambridge. I am bound to say that he is not much liked. However, I find it, ah, difficult to imagine that a man like Tawara might be involved in criminal activities.''

''We'll pass over that just for a moment, Dr Kubo. Let me just remind you that the late Murakami was well-known as an extreme rightist in politics. Let me also remind you that you know and I know that Dr Tawara was in his younger days a militant radical.'' Otani nodded reassuringly at Kubo, then raised an eyebrow to invite a response.

''I can imagine that a person like Murakami might have enemies. It seems to me to be inconceivable that he should be killed in Cambridge of all places, but granted that he was, I suppose it is natural that you should investigate Tawara's background. Of course it has been known for months that Murakami would very probably come to Cambridge for the opening ceremony; and there has been a certain amount of discussion about him in our community here.''

''Yes.''

Kubo waited, as though he expected Otani to say more

than that, then plunged on. "Far be it from me to impugn the character of a colleague, but I must say . . . you have *not* interviewed him yet, I think you said?"

"Not yet." Otani was still idly thumbing through Kubo's passport. "I expect when I do he will make an equally convincing case against you, Dr Kubo." Kubo's face was a mask as Otani went on.

"There are two possible motives for the murder of Shigeru Murakami. One of them is political, and points to Tawara, for reasons which we have just been discussing and which you have encouraged me to think might be sound. But there is another. Here in the Embassy we've been looking at a very interesting telex we received earlier today from Tokyo. From the computer centre at the National Police Agency," he added helpfully, as Kubo made an ineffectual lunge across the desk for his passport, which Otani deftly slipped into his inside pocket.

"Do sit down, Dr Kubo. Let me explain what I know and you are beginning to fear that I have discovered. Needless to say Tawara's record of radical violence is on the computer. It is a fairly conventional one, but one which undoubtedly makes him a suspect in the present case. But your own rather more unusual connections are also recorded, and I have been able to supplement the information on the computer from local sources in my part of Japan. You were that rare animal in the sixties, Dr Kubo, a right-wing militant. You were a graduate student, newly married, surprisingly enough, to the daughter of a rightist politician. The anti-communist faction you organised in Hiroshima gave the police even more trouble than the Maoists, with your mindless violence. You had help from gangsters, both money and weapons, and the funds were forthcoming on ridiculously easy terms from a loan company operated by the *yakuza*. You never really expected to pay the money back, and you never have."

Kubo opened his mouth to speak, but no words came.

"Over the years, though, you've done little jobs for them. You've lived well, and made a respectable academic career. It worried you when the news was announced that Murakami would be coming to Cambridge. You'd been keeping an eye on Tawara anyway, and your rightist friends made it clear that it was up to you to—shall we say, neutralise Tawara, whom they knew all about. Until very recently it was, funnily enough, a question of *protecting* Murakami. You hated Tawara anyway because you knew he'd seduced your daughter." Kubo again tried to speak, but only a choking snarl emerged

"It came as a colossal surprise to you when you received the message from your other friends, the *yakuza* of Hiroshima. You had to adjust to the idea that Murakami, the rightist, had suddenly become inconvenient to them. You were ordered to do the biggest job ever for them. To kill Murakami." Otani looked at the skinny pedantic-looking man gaping at from the other side of the desk and tried to visualise him driving a knife into Murakami's chest.

"What I'm anxious to know is this. Did you do it yourself, or did you thank your lucky stars when Tawara conveniently did it for you?"

Chapter 15
Cambridge

CHIEF SUPERINTENDENT NICKLEBY HUMMED TUNElessly to himself as he sat with Sergeant Farrier in the front of the unmarked car belonging to the Cambridge police: he was himself unaware of doing so, brooding as he was over the implications of the report and recommendations Otani had made with Noda's assistance in the preceding hour. The two Japanese were in the back of the car, parked in a side street not more than a block away from the Low Temperature Research Institute. It was an elderly vehicle, much less impressive than the Rover in which Nickleby had been driven from London that morning, and all at once he turned crossly to Farrier.

"Right old banger you've found us here, lad. Where'd you get it, off the Sally Army?"

"It serves a turn, Guv'nor," Farrier said equably. "I reckon we'd have done better to come in a furniture van anyway. Four blokes in a car—dead suspicious if you ask me."

Otani gazed quietly out of the window during the exchange. Although he did not at all understand what Nickleby and Farrier had said, he felt uneasily conspicuous sitting there, and had said as much to Noda.

The few pedestrians about looked at the car with varying degrees of curiosity, and one old man with a flowing white moustache stared with ostentatious hostility at them as his dog excreted on to the pavement, then took out a small notebook and very carefully entered the registration number of the car before stumping off, having, to Otani's amazement, done nothing to clear up the mess in the road.

"Now look. You quite sure you're happy about this, Mr Noda? I mean, bit of a surprise to me that your Embassy goes along with him being picked up with this sort of hoop-la. I'll take the Superintendent's word for it that he reckons he's got this Tawara bang to rights. I'm looking forward to casting an eye over him myself, but all this is a bit unnecessary if you ask me. Why not wait till he comes out under his own steam after all?" As he spoke Nickleby twisted round in his seat and peered belligerently at the two Japanese.

"No doubt in our minds at all, Chief Superintendent. It was good of you to let Superintendent Otani here carry on with the questioning of Kubo after you arrested him as he left the Embassy. Now you've got his statement, and you can almost certainly nail him as a conspirator, or an accessory before the fact, I think you call it. But having seen Tawara this morning the Superintendent is now quite convinced he actually killed Murakami. Your own people found out Tawara's travel plans by checking the airline offices, but I accept the Superintendent's warning that he may evade us if we don't move fast."

Nickleby seemed disinclined to answer, so Farrier did so, his quiet Fenland accents in contrast to the brisk metropolitan style of the other. "Not quite easy in our minds, we aren't, Mr Noda. I grant you there's a lot of circumstantial evidence against him on top of Kubo's statement. Specially him deciding to up and go all of a sudden. But then he'd have done better to just take himself off to Heathrow and get the first plane he could, not make a reservation through the East Anglia and Global Travel Agency."

Farrier's last words were muffled by a mighty trumpeting from Nickleby as he blew his nose, and Nickleby took up the point on his behalf. "Then again, bold as brass, eh? If he's the villain. Finishing up his experiments first. What does the Super think?" Noda interpreted the sense of the points made by Farrier and Nickleby into Japanese, and Otani pondered before replying.

"Tawara must have known that time was running out for him well before I had my talk with him this morning. He was almost—well, he seemed to be quite enjoying himself with the idea that I didn't believe a word he said, and that the alibi his little girl friend gave him was worthless. He said all the careful things which would protect him, with a smile on his face now and then. Thinking that within a few hours he'd be away from this country no doubt; or out of things, anyway. Of course, he knew Kubo had been arrested, and he might just possibly have thought he was clear, but I doubt it. It's my opinion that he was simply relieved that the months of pressure were over at last, and that he'd come to a point of decision. Tell the Chief Superintendent."

As Noda did so, Otani felt dispirited and at odds with himself, wishing he had never become involved in the affair in the first place. The prospect of action stirred him physically, but the sense of depression and the image of Tawara's detached, amused expression as he had shown Otani out of his small office in the Department of Physics building not far from Corpus Christi College, remained with him. All in all he would almost have preferred to be with Hanae and Akiko, shopping for souvenirs in London.

At first he had made no objection to Nickleby's proposal to wait until Tawara left the Institute to pick him up and take him to Cambridge police Headquarters for formal questioning with Otani as adviser and Noda as his interpreter, but later in the conversation he changed his mind and pressed the counter-suggestion of surprising Tawara at work in the laboratory at the Institute on his final afternoon. It was hard for him to explain his sudden intuitive awareness of Tawara's likely state of mind and the new sense of urgency it stimulated, and he did not do so quite frankly. Noda obviously understood, though, and Otani was glad that Nickleby had eventually agreed. The four men had set out in the car as soon as the Director of the Institute telephoned to say that Tawara had arrived there, but had parked for a few minutes for a final conference. Nickleby stared hard during Noda's translation, bushy eyebrows raised interrogatively, then spoke decisively. "Right then, gentlemen. Give him a nasty turn, shall we?"

By one of those curious coincidences which do occur, all four doors of the car opened at precisely the same moment, and the young man and girl who were approaching on the pavement, their arms entwined about each other, found this phenomenon irresistibly amusing. Laughing helplessly, they reeled about in the path of the four men, pointing in speechless paroxysms of mirth at Otani and Noda in particular.

Disentangling themselves at last, the quartet marched sternly on their way, Nickleby muttering obscure threats and Noda explaining to a puzzled Otani that he had no idea what the young couple found so funny but that whatever it was had been much enhanced by the unexpected apparition of two Japanese. "I don't suppose they realised we're police officers," Otani said, never having had the experience of being viewed as an object of mirth by anyone but Hanae before. "Three of us, that is," he added in deference to Noda's diplomatic status.

"The Director of the Institute wasn't too happy about this when I spoke to him earlier, sir," said Farrier as they went in through the gate and approached the virtually windowless building. "Seems that our man's working on some bit of old glacier sample or something that has to be kept in minus 45 degrees. Said it's impossible to talk in there without a special insulated radio like they have on the Antarctic Survey, and theirs has gone on the blink."

The Director stressed his objections again when he received them in his untidy office. "The Master of St Cuthbert's took me into his confidence, yes, and I do understand the necessity to co-operate with the police," he said after greeting his visitors and smiling timidly at Otani, who remained silent throughout the introductions. "Nevertheless, I cannot see why you wish to confront Dr Tawara in this melodramatic fashion."

Nickleby scratched his head. "Can't actually talk in there, that right, sir?"

"Quite out of the question. The protective clothing required rules it out completely."

"No phone? What happens in an emergency?"

"There's a central alarm bell with a heavy metal bell-push in each very low-temperature room, in case a researcher should feel unwell and need assistance."

"Bit sloppy, these arrangements, if you'll pardon me saying so, Professor. What you need is a closed-circuit TV system, same as they catch shoplifters with. Keep an eye on what's going on. Surprised the unions haven't insisted on it." Nickleby studied the look of mounting distaste on the Director's face for a few seconds, then cleared his throat noisily and went on. "Be that as it may, sir, fact is that these two Japanese gentlemen represent their government, and the Superintendent here considers it important to . . . um . . . import an element of surprise. Element of surprise, that's it, yes. So he'll go in there and fetch him out, then we'd like a word with him ourselves."

The day was mild, almost warm, but Otani began to shiver as soon as he took off his jacket in the changing-room which looked like something from a science fiction film. The bulky padded suit incorporating great bulbous boots was much too big for him, and he found time to wonder whether it really needed to be in a lurid shade of orange like a lifejacket on a ship.

Sergeant Farrier too was assisted into similar gear by a round-eyed young man who seemed to be some kind of technician around the place, and then the strange procession made its way down a concrete staircase into a cavernous basement area with the technician and Nickleby in the lead, Otani and Farrier waddling behind, and Noda bringing up the rear. The white walls were innocent of decoration of any kind and the heavy doors along one wall of the wide corridor with their small observation windows put Otani more in mind of a jail than of a scientific research establishment.

Although he could see Noda and Nickleby huddling into themselves in what must already have been a chilly part of the building, he himself felt extremely stuffy in the ungainly padded suit, and was not looking forward to putting on the extraordinary helmet contrivance he had been given to protect his ears, eyes and nose, and which he carried in his hand. Fortunately, there was no need for breathing apparatus as such: a thick pad like a monstrous surgeon's mask would apparently serve to warm the air he breathed to a tolerable temperature.

The technician paused by one of the doors and launched on some kind of explanation, and Otani waited patiently until Noda interpreted for him. "He's going to take us into one of the other labs where the temperature is only a few degrees below zero, so that we can see the kind of layout. Tawara's lab is similar." The young man grinned as he opened a door and led the way in. He was fine, being dressed in a heavy donkey-jacket, but Nickleby protested vigorously once they were all inside with the door closed. "Do me a favour, son, make it short. Trying to turn Mr Noda and me into a couple of brass monkeys, then?"

The inspection of the lab was indeed brief, but long enough for Otani to take in the simplicity of the windowless room with its single shielded light in the concrete ceiling. There were boxes of what looked like snow heaped casually in one corner, each with a date scribbled on it, and Otani reminded himself to tell Hanae how odd it seemed that snow could be kept in perfectly ordinary cardboard cartons without making them damp and soggy.

Back in the corridor, the technician pointed a few yards ahead, to where a red lamp glowed outside another door. "You got a double door there, gents. That's the minus forty-five room. Coldest lab in the Institute."

Nickleby drew himself up and said "Well, get it over with, Super. Longer we go on the barmier it strikes me. Perishing bloody cold, I am." Noda interpreted decorously and Farrier and Otani put on their helmets and gloves after adjusting the breathing masks. The technician opened the outer door and the two men stepped into a small area with just enough room for both of them, and waited till the heavy door swung to behind them.

A large sign lettered in red confronted them below the observation port in the inner door, and though Otani was unable to read it he took it for granted that it must be a warning about the danger of entering it without proper protective clothing. All at once he was no longer excessively warm and the almost complete absence of humidity made his skin and mouth feel very dry. Farrier peered for several seconds through the mica panel in the door ahead of them, then turned to Otani and raised his mittened hands in a gesture of puzzlement, before indicating that Otani should take a look. He did so. The window was tiny and the mica thick, so it did not offer a full view of the room. The workbench was visible, however, and there was no sign of anyone working at it.

Mimicking Farrier's gesture, Otani stepped back and pointed to the big door handle, a little like that on an aircraft. Farrier hauled it to the open position, then swung the door open and stepped over the sill into the lab. Obscured though his movements were by the padded suit, Otani nevertheless saw Farrier's whole body take on a curious rigidity as he stepped into the room too, remembering to close the door as they had been instructed to do. The deadly bitterness of the cold struck even through the layers of thermal padding, and Otani blundered clumsily against Farrier as he moved round him to see what Farrier was staring at.

Tawara looked surprisingly calm down there against the wall. He still had on his padded suit, which had made it impossible for him to assume the lotus position traditionally prescribed for meditation. He had however managed to kneel before taking off his gloves and helmet and time to arrange his hands in the Buddhist *mudra* of mercy. It was the ice which had formed on his open eyes which gave a glittering intensity to the dead man's stare, and Otani almost instinctively moved to close them before realising that it would not be physically possible to do so. Instead, he tapped Farrier's shoulder and pointed to the work-bench. On it was an envelope, and the two men moved over for a closer look at it. Otani bent to read the inscription on it through his goggles and was not entirely surprised to see that it was addressed, in Japanese, to himself.

Chapter 16

Kobe

"NO POINT IN IT, KIMURA," NOGUCHI PROTESTED once more as they were being driven down to the passenger terminal of the ferry company. Kimura was sporting his uniform again, and kept his braided cap on in the car. His jaw was set, and for once he seemed impervious to Noguchi's assaults, whether they took the form of sarcasm, attempts at sweet reason, or downright invective. "Look, at least let me get on board first and get the kid off."

The driver swung the car round at speed and Kimura clutched at his cap to keep it in position. When he had recovered his poise he looked at Noguchi aloofly. "Officer Migishima seems to have performed very creditably. According to the captain of the ferry, she is perfectly safe under his protection. Indeed there is no evidence that the people on board suspect anything is amiss. They have had their trip, enjoyed themselves presumably, and now have hangovers. A very good time to pick them up."

Then he relented. "Nevertheless, I see your point, Ninja. All right. You go on board and take care of Migishima-san. I'll organise the arrests as they come through one by one. They certainly won't take *you* for a police officer." Although Noguchi was dressed in scruffy clothes of the kind he generally wore, he himself was not so sure. It would only take one or two of the local *yakuza* to spot him for the word to flash round like lightning, but he hoped that by using the crew gangway which gave admittance to the ship one deck below that used by passengers, he could make his way to the officers' quarters aft of the bridge and reassure himself about Junko's safety before Kimura went ahead with his plan to arrest the entire complement of passengers as they disembarked, then to release the girls with a caution before sifting through the haul of gangsters.

Twenty or more plain-clothes officers were already in position at the exit gates, and buses were parked nearby, in such a pattern as to form a kind of compound in which the sheep could be sorted out from the goats. Even Noguchi had to concede that the men would probably go quietly, and unfortunately the plan had the approval of the District Prosecutor, granted as soon as Otani's message had been received from the Japanese Embassy in London. Mass arrests were not Noguchi's way. He would greatly have preferred to take in Shiraishi, Uchibori and the other members of the presidium, leaving lesser hoodlums to be scooped up at leisure and without fuss.

As it was, Noguchi merely grunted in response to Kimura as the driver pulled up at the approach to the jetty. It was used by the ferry company for their scheduled sailings to Shikoku, and the ticket office was open for normal business, with a small queue of outward-bound travellers in front of it. The *Tosa Maru* was in clear view no more than a kilometre out and making for the eastern berth of the double-sided jetty. The ship tied up at the western berth and preparing to sail was only half its size, its passenger accommodation designed for day trips only.

Since there was no question of Customs or other formalities for domestic shipping services, there were no security barriers as such; merely movable railings positioned to enable disembarking passengers to make their way out against the lighter and more sporadic flow of boarding passengers without confusion. The day was very warm, and Kimura mopped the headband of his cap with the handkerchief he kept in his pocket.

After standing beside him looking out at the bustle of Kobe Harbour for a moment or two, Noguchi disappeared. Kimura had known him quite long enough to have seen Noguchi perform this trick many times, but on this occasion he could have sworn that he had actually been looking at Noguchi when in mid-sentence he realised all at once that he was alone. Squinting into the sunshine, Kimura tried to spot his old colleague and tormentor among the people on the jetty, but he was nowhere to be seen.

Kimura felt bereft and disconcerted by the hubbub at the quayside. He had expected something much more orderly and manageable than the confusion of people coming and going which he actually saw. In order to boost his sagging self-confidence he went and barked a few crisp orders to the assistant inspector in charge of the plain-clothes detail.

The knowledge that the Otanis were due to arrive back at Osaka Airport on the next day but one was at once a source of relief and of apprehension to Kimura. Having spoken himself by radio telephone to Junko Migishima late the previous night, he was bursting with pride in the success of his scheme. Although the news from London about Kubo's statement and the contents of the suicide note Tawara had left for Otani had been enough on its own to persuade the District Prosecutor that there were solid grounds for the proposed arrests, Junko's gleeful confirmation that her tape-recording was of satisfactory quality and that Uchibori stood condemned by his own words meant that the police case was watertight.

However, even if he had the entire leadership of the Yamamoto gangster empire under lock and key within the next hour, Kimura was convinced from bitter and repeated experience that Otani would find the whole affair to constitute a treasure house of material for the withering comments and the even more crushing asides which he employed to such effect during their regular conferences.

Yet it would be good to have the Old Man back. Kimura knew that he would never succeed him as head of the Hyogo force. Even if he gained promotion, the new rules meant that he would have to go to another prefectural force somewhere else in the country, or perhaps to the National Police Agency in Tokyo. Otani himself had been appointed just in time to be able to claim preservation of his personal position in Kobe until retirement before the rotation rules took effect some years earlier.

Although Kimura affected to prefer foreign to Japanese ways and to be a liberated urban bachelor of the type idealised in *Playboy* magazine, in fact he revered Otani and was paradoxically confirmed and reassured in his role as disciple by Otani's tart and critical manner. Even when deflated by it he was conscious of Otani's regard.

There was little for Kimura to do personally once the *Tosa Maru* was tied up, but he blinked a few times and took a deep breath to pull himself together as the white-painted ship nudged the bundles of old motor tyres at the jetty and the mooring lines were made fast. Moving quietly so that he was concealed from view by the ticket office, he watched the motorised gangway trundle into place and deckhands secure it to the passenger entrance. He did not see Noguchi make his way up the smaller gangway pushed out unceremoniously from the crew entrance.

During the ship's approach there had been a few passengers on the observation deck, but none were to be seen there during the final few minutes, and soon the first of them began to emerge from the covered gangway. A bedraggled air of revelry was still to be discerned among some of the hardier souls, and a few women clung amorously to the arms of men with whom they had come to "special friendship" understandings during the night. The sharp suits of the men looked crumpled and less impressive in the bright morning light, and most of the girls looked tired and washed-out, even those who had applied fresh make-up.

Kimura turned to watch the exit gate, having satisfied himself that neither Uchibori nor Shiraishi was among the first twenty or so passengers to leave the ship. As the police officers closed in there was at first no more than a minor sense of disturbance, but as soon as a girl's voice was raised in a shrill protest confusion developed rapidly, and soon fistfighting broke out. The plain-clothes men had difficulty in keeping it under control, and Kimura spoke into his radio. No more than a minute later uniformed men swarmed into view and Kimura himself marched out of concealment to take command.

He was tempted to use the loud-hailer, but after a moment's hesitation nodded to the assistant inspector whose amplified voice then boomed out, requiring all passengers disembarking from the *Tosa Maru* to report at the police checkpoint at the jetty. The confusion became greater as some of the yakuza tried to turn in their tracks and go back on board, and a few of the more enterprising made for the Shikoku ferry no more than fifty metres away.

Kimura was finding it increasingly hard to maintain an air of Olympian detachment as policemen darted here and there; and hoped against hope that the repeated warnings over the loud-hailer would soon take effect and that he would not have to call out the squad of riot police on standby in the vicinity.

It was as he was trying to look in several different directions at the same time that Kimura saw Uchibori. Unlike the others making a run for it, Uchibori was sauntering quietly along the jetty in the opposite direction from the exit, and was not making directly for the Shikoku ferry, a few of whose legitimate boarding passengers had already been arrested by mistake and who were protesting loudly while others already on board leant over the rail joining in.

Shouting to the man nearest to him to follow, Kimura made straight for Uchibori and was upon him in seconds. There followed a brief and savage encounter which left Kimura bruised and limping. Kimura was proud of his skill at judo, and at just over forty was in excellent physical condition. There were few in the force who had gone beyond his own third *dan* level, and Uchibori's technique was no match for Kimura's. He was, however, violent almost beyond imagination, and there were moments when the thought flashed through Kimura's mind that he might be killed by one of Uchibori's savage kicks or gougings.

Even when he was quelled by no fewer than three men who came to Kimura's assistance, Uchibori snarled like a wild beast. Panting and dishevelled, Kimura limped heavily along behind the handcuffed boss, the blood roaring in his ears as he gasped for breath, his windpipe sore and his heart pounding. It took a while before he heard his own name being called, and turned his head to peer blearily in the direction from which the sound came.

It was Junko Migishima who was breathlessly appealing to him as she was being hustled forcibly along the quayside by a beefy policeman, struggling furiously as he shoved her forward, half-carrying her in his firm grasp. Noguchi for his part was beyond speech, roaring incoherently as he battled with two others, dragging them along with him as he strove to remain at Junko's side. Exhausted as he was, Kimura managed to put himself in front of the group, and the sight of his uniform was as effective as his hoarse command to the three uniformed officers to release their victims.

Junko was furious. Eyes flashing, she straightened the kimono in which she was still dressed, drew herself up and saluted Kimura. The incongruous gesture finally persuaded the officers of their mistake and they drew back. "Thank you, Inspector," Junko snapped. "If you hadn't come along

I should have been obliged to hurt him." The young man to whom she referred was barely able to stifle the outraged squawk of protest and disbelief that came to his lips but did so and stood red-faced with his colleagues as Noguchi finally found words and treated the trio to one of the most blistering dressings-down Kimura had heard in his entire career.

He was content to let Noguchi have his say. It gave him time to regain his own breath and gingerly explore the damage to his leg; and to notice with satisfaction that some sort of order was beginning to emerge from the former chaos on the quay. Eventually Noguchi was done, and reverted to snorts and growls as Kimura ordered the three patrolmen away. He saw no point in taking their names, and indeed felt a certain fleeting sympathy with them in their discovery that the elderly ruffian and the tattooed bawd were in fact the legendary Ninja Noguchi and a detective officer respectively.

After checking that the crucial tape-recording was in Noguchi's possession and warmly congratulating Junko, Kimura ushered them both towards the car, pausing only to hand over command to the assistant inspector and confirm that Uchibori was already being taken under escort to prefectural headquarters. Kimura wanted very much to witness with his own eyes the arrest of Shiraishi and the rest of the presidium, but had to forgo that pleasure for the greater one of listening to the tape and getting it transcribed so that a written version of Uchibori's confession could be placed in the hands of the District Prosecutor without delay.

Noguchi's rage had expended itself, and on the way to headquarters he was clumsily gentle with Junko. They were sharing the back seat of the car, which Kimura had magnanimously yielded to them. Sitting beside the driver, Kimura pretended not to listen as Noguchi with elephantine tact elicited from Junko the reassuring news that no, she hadn't had to . . . that is, Uchibori hadn't actually . . . that she was very tired but otherwise perfectly all right.

Kimura had deliberately sent her husband on an assignment

in the city of Himeji, but had no idea whether Junko had told him in advance about her planned undercover voyage with the yakuza. It came as a relief to him when as they got out of the car after arriving at the main entrance to the old headquarters building Junko shyly detained him and Noguchi and asked them not to let Migishima know the full story.

Half an hour later they met in Otani's room. Junko was now obviously bathed and refreshed, and had put on the uniform she now so rarely wore. It made her look young and earnest, and bereft of her wig she was virtually unrecognisable as the same woman who had stepped off the ship. Kimura too felt much better after a shower and a change of clothes, into one of his nattiest outfits, an extremely expensive ensemble from Sanohe boutique in Motomachi which handled the exclusive designs of Georgio Armani of Milano. The contusions on his leg stung horribly from the antiseptic fluid with which he had doused them, and his abdomen felt very tender, but he had concluded that Uchibori had done him no lasting harm.

"In spite of her tiredness, Officer Migishima has kindly agreed to make an oral report now, after we all listen to the tape she made. We will tape her report and then she may amend the transcript for the record in any way she sees fit after taking a day or two of well-earned leave."

Kimura looked at the other two, bright-eyed and expectant as he reached to switch on the machine on the coffee table between them, but Noguchi raised a massive hand. It was an economical gesture involving a movement of less than an inch, but it stopped Kimura dead. "Been in the duty room?" Kimura shook his head. "Message from London. The Superintendent's coming back a day early. Be here tomorrow." Noguchi actually beamed with pleasure as he opened his hand and gestured to Kimura to play back Junko's tape.

Chapter 17

Cambridge

"NOT VERY MANY YEARS AGO, MY DEAR LADY, I should not have been able to invite you to be with us this evening," said the Master to Hanae as the soup plates were removed. He raised his glass of white wine and waited politely until she followed suit, then sipped delicately. "It is only in recent years that ladies have graced our High Tables and, in doing so, made us regret the poverty of our former custom." His mellifluous Japanese was like balm to Hanae's soul as she turned to him in relief. The young Fellow on her right had intended, she supposed, to be thoughtful in speaking to her in English very slowly and very loudly, but that merely enhanced her misery in not being able to understand him. This had made her smile all the more brilliant and more fixed as she nodded eagerly, her eyes on his tangled brown beard. It was delightful after such an ordeal to be able to communicate in a civilised manner with Sir Benjamin Lincoln.

"My husband and I are greatly honoured to be here," she said. "Also our daughter and her husband. It is the first time for us all to experience such a traditional English meal.'' The Master chuckled as she glanced along the table to where Akiko and Akira Shimizu were sitting. Akiko was resplendent but ill at ease in a kimono, unlike Hanae who knew she looked her best in her own that evening, while the menfolk were both wearing hired dinner jackets.

In fact Hanae had worked very hard to overcome her daughter's initial refusal to even contemplate encasing herself in the formal Japanese dress she disliked so much, and Otani had not been much help during the argument by pointing out that everyone knew that the Emperor himself steadfastly refused to wear anything but Western-style suits. Eventually, after gently pointing out objections to each of the three long dresses Akiko possessed and stressing the ritual, almost symbolically Anglo-Japanese nature of the coming formal dinner at St Cuthbert's, Hanae had prevailed, and coaxed a mutinous Akiko into one of the several beautiful kimonos she kept folded and stored away, almost forgotten in her new English environment.

''Hardly 'traditional', I fear,'' the Master said. ''Still to some extent customary in the ancient universities and certain other odd corners like the Inns of Court.'' Sir Benjamin had trouble rendering this into Japanese and launched into a short lecture on the habits of English barristers which Hanae happily ignored as she apparently hung on his words while in fact admiring her husband, who was talking animatedly to his neighbour Noda.

Otani was enjoying himself hugely, and as the dinner proceeded on its stately course felt more and more at home in the panelled Hall of St Cuthbert's. It had been more than something of a squeeze to fit in the visit to the formal wear rental shop with Shimizu after the long and final conference at Scotland Yard with Nickleby and Noda, and the courtesy call on the Japanese Ambassador following that.

He had not in fact been entirely convinced that such formal dress was essential for dinner as guest of the Master of St Cuthbert's until the hire car deposited the four of them at the Master's Lodge and they were greeted by Sir Benjamin who was not only wearing an old-fashioned dinner jacket and dress shirt with a wing collar, but a dusty black academic gown over it.

All the other men gathered for sherry were similarly arrayed, and Hanae whispered to Akiko as she spotted one or two ladies with gowns of the same type over their long dresses. It looked very odd indeed, but nobody else seemed to find it so as they chatted until the butler made a mysterious announcement and everyone trooped through the cloisters into Hall.

Having spent the greater part of the day in discussing the ramifications of the case with Nickleby, Noda and the Ambassador, Otani gradually disengaged the conversation over dinner and plied Noda with questions about university life in England, gazing interestedly as he ate and drank at the serried ranks of young men and women in their black gowns below and in front of them.

Later, he was quite unable to remember what he had eaten, but the scene in Hall remained in his memory always, especially when the Master stood and everyone else scrambled to follow his example. Otani wondered for a moment if there was a fire, though there seemed to be no note of urgency in Sir Benjamin's voice as he mumbled a few completely incomprehensible words in a language which was certainly not Japanese and did not sound like English either. Nevertheless, what could only be thought of as a stampede ensued among the undergraduates and they nearly all left the premises before the occupants of High Table had begun to make their way more sedately off the dais.

Otani had been looking forward to being reunited with Hanae at the conclusion of the meal, and was disappointed when he saw her being shepherded firmly away in the company of the other ladies by a fierce elderly woman, while he and the other men were led in a different direction by the Master, into a room dominated by a huge polished table surrounded by a great many chairs. Rather bemused, and keeping close to Noda and Shimizu, Otani settled himself down and watched the Master remove the stoppers from two cut-glass decanters and sniff gently at their contents. It was as he was doing this that Noda explained to Otani that the language the Master had used for the benediction in Hall was Latin.

Noda then gestured at the decanters. "The red one's port," he whispered. "I'm not sure what the other is."

"Madeira," Sir Benjamin said, smiling in their direction as he passed the two decanters to the decrepit old man on his left, whose dinner jacket bore patches of what looked uncommonly like green mould. Otani watched with interest as the decanters made the round of the table, and chose Madeira when they reached him, mainly because he noticed that there was rather more left than remained of the port. There followed a cryptic exchange between two men who had taken no part in the proceedings until that point, and which sounded to Otani like a brief private conversation but which Noda said was some kind of toast involving the Queen and the Church, and they all sipped.

Although the three Japanese had sat together out of an instinctive sense of group solidarity, both Shimizu and Noda fell into conversation with their English neighbours, leaving Otani in the middle beginning to become slightly bored and more than a little sleepy, until he was brought back to full consciousness by the crystalline tinkle of the Master's glass as he gently tapped it with his cheese knife.

Sir Benjamin inclined his head courteously towards Otani as he began to speak in English, quite obviously about him, since all the faces round the table turned in his direction, bearing expressions ranging from Shimizu's broad grin to puzzlement in the case of the old man on the Master's left. Seeing Noda beginning to whisper a translation to Otani, the Master raised a thin hand and stopped him, then himself switched to Japanese.

"I have been explaining to my colleagues and our guests how greatly the College community is indebted to you, Otani-san, for the professional skill and personal sensitivity with which you have assisted us over the distressing events of the past week or so. It is indeed unfortunate that the opening of our magnificent new Institute for Japanese Studies has been clouded by tragedy and worse. Nevertheless, I am quite sure that thanks largely to you, the affair has been dealt with both effectively and expeditiously. You take with you on your departure from these shores our respectful goodwill, and I wish you to know that henceforth you will always be a most welcome guest at our table."

After continuing in this vein for some time, the Master looked round for the butler, who stepped forward with a package in his hands and passed it to Sir Benjamin with immense gravity. "I therefore request you to accept this small token of fellowship and appreciation," he concluded as Otani got to his feet and bowed, before moving round to the Master and receiving the package.

Sir Benjamin's most honorific Japanese was so flowery that both Shimizu and Otani himself could be forgiven their misapprehension. In the car going back to London at the end of the evening, as Hanae and Akiko admired the wooden plaque bearing the painted heraldic device of St Cuthbert's and the silk tie with the diagonal purple and grey stripes which was undoubtedly of the same pattern as those worn by many of the participants in the opening ceremony which seemed to have taken place such aeons before, Otani explained proudly and Shimizu confirmed that he had been made an honorary member of the College. "Would it be like an emeritus professor in Japan?" Hanae asked in awe, her eyes wide.

Otani shrugged with poorly feigned nonchalance. "Something like that," he agreed.

Even Akiko was impressed, and they were all chattering happily as they tumbled out of the car at last at St John's Wood and Shimizu let them into the flat, where a drowsy Rosie blinked as she reported an uneventful evening. Roger was with her, and proved to be a lanky young man whose beard was even more luxuriant than that of the Fellow of St Cuthbert's who had sat next to Hanae at dinner. As introductions were made Hanae tried very hard not to notice that Rosie's blouse had been rebuttoned wrongly and that there were livid red tooth-marks on Roger's neck.

Furthermore, she hoped that Rosie's comprehension of Japanese was not so good as to enable her to grasp the purport of the effusive remarks that her husband was making as he shook Roger's hand and smiled at the pair of them. Hanae could quite understand the expansiveness of Otani's mood, but inviting young English girls and their bearded bus-conductor lovers to stay with them in their house at Rokko was a sign that he must be over-tired, over-excited, or both.

Chapter 18
Rokko

"WHAT A SURPRISE TO FIND SO MANY PEOPLE WAITing for us!" Hanae said happily as she turned to give a final wave to the group of bowing figures outside the international arrivals wing at Itami Airport, Osaka. The car was held up briefly on the turn leading to the Meishin Expressway, and Otani bent forward to wave as well so that they could see him. He noticed that Kimura had already straightened up and was looking at his watch, though Noguchi's head was still lowered.

Then Tomita the driver was able to reach the toll-booth and be waved through by the attendant, and Otani sank back gratefully into the familiar upholstery of the Toyota Police Special. "Yes. I was glad to see the Migishimas there. And you, of course, Tomita-kun," he added hastily to the back of the driver's head. Hanae took up the brief litany of appreciation and in response to Tomita's polite questions gave him an account of the weather conditions in England and agreed that they were a *little* tired and very happy to be home again. Hanae had a special present for Tomita; shortbread in a tin decorated with a Scottish tartan.

She intended to hand it over to him when they arrived at Rokko.

"And all those people at Narita," she continuted to Otani when honour was satisfied in respect of Tomita. This time Otani merely grunted. During the two hours they had waited at Tokyo's new and spectacularly inconvenient airport fifty miles from the city for one of the few domestic flights from there to Osaka he had spent a full hour in conference in one of the VIP rooms with three senior officers of the National Police Agency and a shadowy figure who admitted to being from the Public Security Investigation Agency but who had not done Otani the courtesy of offering him his name-card. When he thought about it, Otani realised that it would be somewhat eccentric for a member of the Japanese secret service to go about leaving evidence of his identity with all and sundry, but the matter rankled a little just the same.

Hanae was not offended in the least by having been excluded from the conference. She knew well enough that now they were back in Japan, her husband would revert to his normal, self-contained manner and would not reveal as he had in England any doubts or hesitations connected with his work. Although the thought made her a little sad, it had all the same been a real pleasure to her to wander about listening to the sound of Japanese voices again, to watch the tour groups being marshalled by young women with flags upraised, and to spend twenty minutes at the newspaper kiosk looking through the new *Katei Gaho* and other women's magazines.

The men in dark business suits who had been waiting in the big circular transit lounge and who intercepted Otani as soon as he and Hanae emerged from the airbridge tunnel from the JAL jumbo jet had pretty much ignored her, except for Senior Superintendent Nitta of the NPA whom she had met once at a reception in Tokyo in honour of a retiring Superintendent General. His rubbery face split into a fat, jolly smile and they even exchanged a few words before Hanae somehow found herself alone with a JAL ground hostess who whisked her through a back corridor and into the public area of the terminal building. The young woman might indeed have become a burden to Hanae, since she showed every sign of planning to remain at her side until the onward flight to Osaka was called. Realising this, Hanae had gently but firmly dismissed her, taking possession of her boarding card and promising not to be late.

"There were one or two things to talk about," Otani said after a while, and Hanae knew he would say little more until they were alone together, if then. Then he turned to her and smiled in a way that all at once made him look much younger. "You know, because of that, we never did go through Customs, did we?" He cleared his throat and addressed Tomita in mock-official tones. "Do not misunderstand me, Tomita," he said. "I should not wish you to imagine that I would attempt to introduce contraband articles into this country. However . . ." He reached into his flight bag and took out a boxed bottle of Dimple Haig whisky and reached over to place it on the passenger seat beside Tomita, winking solemnly as he caught the driver's eye in the rear-view mirror.

Tomita tried to respond in an appropriately dead-pan way but was incapable, and was still babbling his thanks as they left the expressway at Nishinomiya and he piloted the Otanis up through the familiar streets leading to the foothills of Mount Rokko and their house. Otani was briefly tempted to show Hanae the copy of the uncensored *Playboy* magazine he had bought for Kimura at London Airport, but thought better of it. It was rather pointless anyway: police officers in Japan who had a taste for unretouched nude photographs never had any trouble in getting hold of them. It was the man in the street who had to supply in imagination what was obliterated by black squares painted on imported magazines by teams of housewives working part-time in Yokohama Customs House.

He had whisky for Kimura too, of course, and for Noguchi, though Otani doubted if he would drink it himself since he preferred sake or the sometimes villainous *shochu* spirit. Otani was tired, in spite of their having been treated by the stewardesses on the long JAL flight as though they had been members of the Imperial Family. Images and impressions of their stay in Britain crowded his mind, and he would have liked another holiday to give himself time to assimilate them; yet here it was after five o'clock already. Time for a good night's rest, but with a conference agreed with Kimura and Noguchi for the next morning at ten, official concerns would crowd in on him soon enough.

It seemed Kimura had done well, on the whole, and Otani was more than ready to set in train the paperwork which would result in a citation for him and a promotion for Officer Migishima. He hoped that the latter distinction wouldn't make her husband jealous. The follow-up work on the Tawara suicide would fall to the Nara Prefectural Police, and since the interests of the two main rivals like those of the other lesser barons of the former Yamamoto empire spread over a number of prefectures, Otani had been glad enough to agree to transfer responsibility to the National Police Agency. Nitta was a crafty, experienced man, and he knew how to handle the spooks of the Public Security Investigation Agency.

The Yamamoto crime syndicate would certainly not go away, and there would be plenty for Noguchi to do in Kobe. Kimura too could profitably be set to work investigating the network of organisations under the Murakami Foundation umbrella: even during their brief conversation at Osaka Airport while Tomita was putting their suitcases in the car Kimura had burbled about some mystery woman he had met at the Foundation, and Otani concluded that since Kimura had been smitten by her he would no doubt go prowling around her anyway. He might just as well do so with Otani's knowledge and approval and therefore some chance of being rendered accountable.

"Has it really been less than two weeks?" Otani rattled the outer gate open and fumbled for his key as Hanae looked up at the shuttered house. They hardly ever pulled the heavy wooden *amado* storm shutters into place over the windows except once or twice a year in the typhoon season, or if they were away for more than a day or two. The shutters had made the inside of the old house very dark, and by unspoken agreement they ignored the prospect of mail in the box and, pausing only to slip off their shoes, set to work to open up the windows, Hanae upstairs and Otani down.

"Hot compared to England, isn't it?" he called up to her when he had finished and taken their luggage from Tomita who brought it to the door and was standing waiting for his orders for the next morning. Hanae replied, but Otani couldn't catch what she said. She sounded cheerful, anyway. "Eight o'clock, I think," he decided after a while. It might be useful to have half an hour or so to collect his thoughts at the office before the others arrived.

Tomita had gone and Otani was moving about the downstairs all-purpose room plugging in the television and small electric fan when Hanae came down wearing a cotton yukata and started to fill the bath with very hot water. The sound of it filled him with pleasure. It would be good to have a proper bath again instead of the unsatisfactory ablutions he had been obliged to contrive in the Shimizus' ultramodern bathroom in London. He went upstairs himself, leaving a trail of discarded clothing in his wake, and looked appreciatively round the room in which he and Hanae slept and which served also as their reception room on the rare occasions when they had guests. Hanae had not only thrown back the wooden storm shutters but had opened the paper shoji screens and the glass windows behind which Otani remembered as having been such an innovation when old Professor Otani had had them installed soon after the war.

The slender, stripped and polished trunk of a cryptomeria tree which formed the frame of the *tokonoma* alcove was as old as the house, and Otani ran his hand lovingly over the silky wood as he puzzled briefly once more over the possible meaning of the Chinese calligraphy on the scroll which hung in the alcove, while he savoured the feeling of the tatami matting under his bare feet.

To make his contentment even greater, Hanae washed his back for him as he sat on the tiny blue plastic stool in the bathroom before rinsing himself off and lowering himself into the deep square tub and squatting there immersed to the chin, a small hand-towel balanced on top of his head. He almost, but not quite, persuaded Hanae to allow him to wash her in turn, but eventually she shooed him away.

Philosophically, Otani tied his sash round his waist and straightened his yukata before pottering out of the back door to have a look at his small collection of bonsai miniature trees, and was still absorbed in trimming a minute, perfectly-shaped maple when Hanae came out and joined him in the warm evening air.

They had already decided to have *sushi* for supper, and the question for decision was whether to telephone the *sushi* shop and have it delivered by one of the assistants on his motor scooter, or go down the hill and eat it on the premises. Hanae would not dream of allowing herself to be seen in public in a yukata except at a hot-spring resort hotel, but Otani frequently went out for an evening stroll thus attired, and decided in the end that he would go and fetch their boxes of *sushi* for the sake of the exercise.

Hanae accompanied him to the front door, and sank unselfconsciously to her knees as Otani rooted out a pair of wooden *geta* sandals from the box in the porch and slipped them on his feet to replace the old ones he had been wearing in the tiny garden and which stayed permanently outside the back door. The *geta* for use in public were much better-looking, the smooth pawlonia wood of expensive quality and the thongs of fine padded velvet.

Otani checked the sleeve of his yukata to make sure that his cigarettes and lighter were safely stowed there: he was trying to cut down on his smoking by restricting it to the open air. Hanae passed him a five-thousand yen note and he bowed slightly to her as he took it.

"*Itte kimasu.*"

"*Itte irasshai.*" They had exchanged the farewell salutation many thousands of times over their years together, but Hanae always felt slightly forlorn when she saw her husband go. She shook her head with a hint of impatience at her own foolishness. He would be back in an hour with the two neatly-wrapped boxes of slabs of raw fish nestling snugly on their patties of dressed rice, little seaweed-wrapped rolls of the same rice with a core of cucumber or tuna-fish, some blush-pink pickled ginger in one corner, and throwaway chopsticks in paper wrappers tucked into the string. He would almost certainly have eaten two or three pairs of sushi up at the counter while waiting for their order to be made ready, washing them down with green tea and glancing at the television mounted high in one corner of the small shop.

Or very likely a beer, Hanae mused as she moved about the familiar house, their "rabbit hutch" as Akira Shimizu had teasingly called it during the farewells at London Airport while the tears which she forbade herself to shed stung at Hanae's eyes and Otani hugged young Kazuo rather too hard, so that the little boy yelped in protest.

The weeks to come would not be easy for her. While her husband fell contentedly back into his official surroundings with Kimura and Noguchi to help tease out the implications of the death of the daimyo and the murder of his secret partner, Hanae knew she would be haunted by the silly, miserably unhappy face of Mrs Kubo. She would wonder endlessly whether Tawara bad written a farewell note to poor Tomoko, for Hanae had not forgotten that young love is often tragically intense. She would visualise the loneliness and shame of mother and daughter as Kubo's involvement was investigated and retribution followed, and often blame herself for being even marginally responsible for so much misery.

All the same, it was good to be home.

Chapter 19

Kobe

AS HE MADE HIS WAY ALONG THE DISMAL CORRIDOR towards his office, Otani looked for the first time in many months at the strip of coconut matting laid down the centre of the shiny brown linoleum and decided that something would have to be done about it. It would be decidedly embarrassing if his new friend Chief Superintendent Nickleby *were* to pay him the visit Otani had so warmly urged, and see the holes and frayed edges.

The framed photographs of his predecessors in office since the establishment of prefectural police forces in Japan in the late nineteenth century, on the other hand, impressed Otani every time he passed them; and he quite looked forward to the day when his own likeness would hang at the end of the line of mutton-chop whiskers, soup-strainer moustaches and glum expressions. He would, he thought, be depicted in civilian dress.

He opened the door of his office and stood for a moment savouring the feeling of being back. With part of his mind Otani was conscious of the absurdity of making so much of it after an absence of a mere two weeks; though oddly enough he had never previously been away so long since his appointment to the post. Like the majority of salaried officials, Otani seldom took holidays of more than two or three days at a time, and his absences on official business were usually even briefer.

It was the effect of having been abroad that made him see the familiar office with new eyes, and he was disturbed by its spartan bleakness. Nickleby's office at Scotland Yard had been carpeted wall to wall. Otani sighed, and put the idea firmly out of his mind. The prefectural government might be talked into building a brand-new headquarters of the flashy kind they had in neighbouring Osaka; but Otani was quite sure that money would not be forthcoming to transform his existing office into something more like that of the manager of a better-class hotel.

Otani was glad to have arrived early, and spent a few minutes aimlessly wandering round the room, pausing at one moment to sniff suspiciously. There was something like a hint of perfume lingering in the air. Surely Kimura hadn't . . . ? Otani could believe most things of him, but doubted whether he would go to the extreme of conducting an amorous tryst in the office of his commander.

After straightening the gloomy painting which hung on the wall and which Otani felt that the Master of St Cuthbert's might well appreciate were he to change his mind and visit Japan one day, he went at last to his desk and sat down experimentally. The in-tray was full, but not outrageously so, the out-tray empty. The one in the centre which bore the Chinese characters which mean ''Undecided'' contained a single file, entitled Murakami Foundation.

Before settling down to read it, Otani opened the drawer in which he normally put his lacquer lunch box, and was startled to find much of the space occupied by a gold-braided uniform hat, which he removed and studied. It was in nearly new condition but had obviously been worn. Inside was a label inscribed in black ink, ''Acting Commander Kimura''.

After a period of silent contemplation Otani placed the hat carefully to one corner of the desk and rummaged further. Underneath where the hat had been were two letters. One was in an airmail envelope and Otani was able to read the typewritten address without too much difficulty. Although he detested the Roman alphabet he had of course been obliged to learn it as a child, and he mouthed the sounds as he picked out ''Jiro Kimura'' and noted that the letter had been posted in Bonn in Germany. He supposed that ''Trudi Blohm'' must be one of Kimura's former girl friends among the foreign Consular Corps.

The other was much easier, being addressed to Kimura in Japanese. The sender was, needless to say, another woman, writing from an address in Akashi to the west of Kobe. Otani up-ended Kimura's cap and placed the two letters carefully inside, making no attempt to read them. The only other alien objects in his desk drawer were a plastic box of visiting cards describing Jiro Kimura as a member of the planning and project section of the Dentsu Advertising Agency, a pair of disposable chopsticks and one of the new low-priced digital wristwatches incorporating an electronic game. Otani raised his eyes at the last in particular. Vastly popular though they were among teenagers, such a toy was hardly Kimura's style. He would be more likely to acquire one which could give the time of the day in New Delhi and the phases of the moon.

All of Kimura's property was reposing inside the hat and Otani was buried in the report on the Murakami Foundation by the time the door was opened without a warning tap and Noguchi walked in. Although they had spoken briefly the previous afternoon at the airport, Otani stood up and the two men made a small ceremony of their reunion, Noguchi professing pleased surprise on receiving his bottle of whisky and even producing a connected sentence or two of formal welcome.

Kimura arrived shortly after that, as Otani was assuring Noguchi with thanks that not only Hanae but also their daughter, grandson and son-in-law were in excellent health. Otani treated him with the same bland courtesy, savouring without change of expression the look in Kimura's eye as he spotted the uniform cap full of bric-à-brac on the corner of the desk. Kimura too having received his present, the three sat down in their usual chairs, and silence fell.

This was nothing unusual in the case of Noguchi, but Kimura generally had plenty to say for himself, and Otani wondered what was stopping him, until he realised that he was guilty of a real discourtesy to Kimura. He had, after all, designated him as Acting Commander during his absence, and the man had a right to make his handover report without the sardonic presence of Noguchi in the background. He therefore hastily made amends.

"I shall, of course, want a private conference with you this morning, Kimura-kun," he said. "I thought that before formally resuming command, though, I should report to you both about my activities in England, especially since I had to answer a lot of questions about them when I met some NPA people at Narita Airport on our way back here."

Mollified at once, Kimura sat back gracefully as Otani went on to give a skilfully economical account of his involvement in the Murakami murder case as seen from the English end. Otani was serious, straightforward and businesslike, scarcely interrupting his account when his clerk brought in green tea on the familiar battered tin tray, even though he managed to empty and re-fill his cup several times from the kettle before he had finished. He was scrupulous to say nothing about events in Kobe, but the fiction that Kimura had not yet relinquished command to him became more and more transparent as the minutes ticked by.

Otani fell silent at last. There followed a pause, during

which Noguchi grunted, and Kimura examined his fingernails. ‘‘Well, Ninja. Thank you for joining us. Perhaps we might have a bite of lunch together later? I didn't bring any with me today.'' Otani smiled at his old friend as Noguchi lumbered to his feet, and winked at him almost imperceptibly. He knew that Noguchi was not in the least offended at being dismissed from the room, and also that over a bowl of Chinese noodles he would learn anything he needed to know and which Kimura didn't see fit to tell him. He could also thank him for piecing together the vital information about Kubo's past.

Left alone with Kimura, Otani surveyed him thoughtfully, from the top of his head to his expensively shod feet, then fixed Kimura's bright black diamond eyes with his own. ‘‘Well, Inspector,'' he said at last. ‘‘I see you're admiring my tie.''

Kimura blinked and nodded immediately. ‘‘It's a splendid tie. Rather like the one the Scotland Yard man gave you at the Interpol conference,'' he said unctuously.

‘‘Oh this is rather more special'' Otani said airily. ‘‘Cambridge University, you know. They made me a member.'' On the way to the office Otani had silently rehearsed a few world-weary, jet-set remarks in order to impress Kimura with a cosmopolitan nonchalance equal to his own, but when it came to the point it seemed scarcely worth the effort.

‘‘I brought you an extra present, Kimura-kun,'' he said instead, as Kimura gaped in awe at the St Cuthbert's tie, and went over to his desk to fetch the uncensored *Playboy* he had smuggled into and out of the house unbeknown to Hanae. ‘‘I thought you might need a little relaxation after all your hard work lately. Oh, and I think these are yours?'' The bulky magazine in one hand, the cap and its contents in the other, he returned to his easy-chair by the coffee table.

Kimura simpered uneasily. "Thank you very much. Er, by the way, Chief, I can explain . . ."

"No need. No need at all." Otani's manner had taken on that blandness which Kimura dreaded above all his other moods. "Oh, and by the way. I'd rather you didn't call me 'Chief. They have a much better expression at Scotland Yard. Would you mind addressing me as 'Guv'nor' in future?"

"Gabunaa?" Kimura reproduced Otani's pronunciation perfectly.

"Please. I'd like that, Kimura."

Baffled but obedient, Kimura proceeded to makc his report.

ABOUT THE AUTHOR

James Melville was born in London in 1931 and educated in North London. He read philosophy at Birkbeck College before being conscripted into the RAF, then took up schoolteaching and adult education. Most of his subsequent career has been spent overseas in cultural diplomacy and educational development, and it was in this capacity that he came to know, love, and write about Japan and the Japanese. He has two sons and is married to a singer-actress. He continues to write more mystery novels starring Superintendent Otani.